Billy Elliot

Billy Elliot

A novel

Melvin Burgess

Based on a motion picture
screenplay by
Lee Hall

W F HOWES LTD

This large print edition published in 2008 by
W F Howes Ltd
Unit 4, Rearsby Business Park, Gaddesby Lane,
Rearsby, Leicester LE7 4YH

1 3 5 7 9 10 8 6 4 2

First published in the United Kingdom in 2001 by
The Chicken House

A CIP catalogue record for this book is available
from the British Library

ISBN 978 1 40742 811 6

Typeset by Palimpsest Book Production Limited,
Grangemouth, Stirlingshire
Printed and bound in Great Britain
by MPG Books Ltd, Bodmin, Cornwall

FSC
Mixed Sources
Product group from well-managed
forests and other controlled sources
Cert no. SGS-COC-2953
www.fsc.org
© 1996 Forest Stewardship Council

BILLY

He's an idiot, my brother, I hate him. He's got good taste in music, though. He always listens to it on his headphones when I'm around so's I can't hear it. Like he owns the air or something. He'd wrap the music up and stick it up his arse if he could.

I don't get much time on my own lately except first thing in the morning before school when me dad and Tony are out on the picket line. It was better when they were working. I could get back from school and I'd have hours to listen to anything I wanted. Nan likes the music too. Dad thinks it's modern rubbish, but she's too old to care about that sort of thing. She never tells on me. She probably can't remember long enough to know what we were doing, anyhow. As soon as Dad and Tony are out the house, I put the music on while I do breakfast. She can't keep her feet still. I can hear her singing along while she's still in bed. Sometimes she gets up and we jiggle around the room together. She does these poses with her arms in the air, trying to balance on one leg and spin round like a ballet dancer – except she's getting on for eighty and can't walk all that well these days, let alone dance.

'Go for it, Nan! Boogie-woogie!'

Me, Dad and Tony try to stop her because they think she's making a fool of herself. Well, but who's to see her? It's just us, we're her family. If she can't make a fool of herself in front of her family, where can she? She should be allowed to dance and listen to music all day long if she wants too, but my brother's too mean to let anyone hear anything except the sound of his voice.

'I danced myself right out the womb,
I danced myself right out the womb.
Is it strange to dance so soon?
I danced myself right out of the womb.'

You know? It fills up the whole house. And, oh, man, it was just . . . lovely.

I began to dance round the table while I put the eggs in, pretending to play the guitar. That music just makes you move. Me and my best friend Michael, we used to pretend to be rock stars when we were younger. Michael used to dress up in his sister's satin pyjamas – you know, glam rock – and put on make-up and stuff so he looked like Bowie or Marc Bolan. I didn't care about looking like anyone; I just liked the music. It was great. I used to call him a gay lord and he'd jump on me and try to give me a battering.

'Cosmic Boogie' lasts just long enough to do the

eggs soft – the way my nan likes 'em. I took them out, put them in the eggcups, set out the tray all nice and all. Then I picked the lot up, slid the door to her room to one side with me foot, and I went boogieing into her room.

'Whey-hey, Nan, it's the dancing waiter!' I jiggled in there, doing my best to keep the eggs on their feet . . . and the bloody old thing wasn't there.

Shite! I banged down the tray and ran out the door. Me dad'll kill me if I lose me nan. She disappeared for a whole morning once. The police picked her up in the end wandering around the railway station in Jesmond. How the hell she got there God only knows. Dad thinks she was probably trying to visit someone who'd been dead about fifty years.

I pelted out the back gate and up the road yelling 'Nan! Nan!' at the top of my voice. She frightens the life out of me, Nan. She can't look after herself. You turn your back for a minute and poof! – she's not there. It isn't that she moves all that fast, you wonder how she gets so far. Once she gets going, she just never stops.

I could bloody kill her! I had to get to school. But, well. It's not her fault she's old, is it?

Which way, which bloody way? She might have gone down to the sea. You can see the sea from where we are. Sometimes she goes down and watches the waves. I stood there looking first one way, then the other. Where? But there was

3

little Alison from a few doors down sucking a rusk or something, and she pointed her finger uphill.

I went haring off. If Nan had gone that way, I had a good idea where she was.

I was bloody knackered by the time I got there, but there she was, all right, in the field under the viaduct. I knew it. She always goes there, it's bloody awful: there's a pond, she could fall in and drown. No one knows why she goes there – no one knows why she does anything, really. If you ask her, she just looks at you. I reckon she used to play there as a kid. She's lived here all her life. Eighty years. Eighty years! Christ!

'Nan!' I yelled. She turned and stared at me. I pushed up through the long grass. It was soaking. Poor old thing, she was wet through. She looked terrified. That's the trouble, see, it's not just us that don't know what she's doing half the time – it's her as well. She frightens herself worse than anyone.

'What about your eggs?' I said.

'You're new,' she said.

'Nan, it's Billy. Billy.'

She nodded and smiled vaguely.

I remember that morning, this is why: on the bridge that cuts across the end of the field three black vans pulled up and the police started to climb out. It was like something out of Dr Who – the vans just kept pouring policemen out of the back of them, like beetles coming out of a crack in the ground. They had these big plastic shields

4

and batons. They looked like something out of the movies.

Nan saw me looking up and looked up too. 'What are they?' she said.

'Police, Nan. It's the police.'

'Bastards!' She shook her fist at them. 'Bastards!' she screamed. Some of them looked down, but we were too far off for them to bother with.

'Have they come for us, Billy?' she whispered. She may be a silly old woman, but she's seen all sorts, my nan. She was alive in the thirties and during the war. She's seen everything. She knows all about the police. She knows whose side they're on.

'Not us, Nan, they're not interested in us.'

'Is it Jackie? Is it Tony?' she asked. I didn't answer. Sometimes my nan scares me more when she knows what's going on. I took her by the arm and led her back home.

I was picking out the tune of 'Cosmic Boogie' on the piano and thinking about Mam. Tony was running about the kitchen slapping slices of bread and marge down his throat and fondling his placards. 'No surrender!' 'Thatcher out!' 'SCAB! SCAB! SCAB!' Dad was fussing – doing the dishes, trying to wipe the floor, putting the cups back in the cupboard. Susan from down the road – Susan Spanners we call her, because of her face – she comes in and does a bit of housework from time to time. Nan was sitting on her bed in her room next door, singing along. Singing something, anyhow, but I don't think it was what I was playing.

Mam's been dead two years now. I don't think anyone remembers my mam except for me any more. I miss her, I miss her every day. People don't see how I miss her, but I do. I miss her when I'm looking in the mirror and when I'm walking through the doors from room to room, or when I'm mucking about on the piano. I think to myself, Well, her fingers would have held that doorknob when she opened it. I remember her in all sorts of ways like that. How she used to do her make-up in the mirror in the hall on her way out when she was in a hurry. There's a little box under the mirror where she used to keep her stuff. There's some lipstick things still in there, actually. It smells just a little how my mam used to smell, but it's stale now. When I look in that mirror, I some-times wonder, if I stare long enough, will I see her face? I've stared for ages before now, trying to see her face inside mine. If you stare long enough, your face seems to change and it scares me half to death. Remembering and missing aren't exactly the same thing, but they're pretty close, and you can't do one without the other.

I've a letter from my mam that she wrote ages ago. Listen.

'Dear Billy.'

Can you hear? Can you hear me mam's voice? Listen. 'Dear Billy, I know I must seem like a distant memory to you. Which is probably a good thing. It will have been a long time. And I will have missed seeing you grow, missed you crying and laughing and shouting and I will have missed telling you off. But please know that I was always there with you all through everything. And I always will be. And I am proud to have known you. And I am proud that you were mine. Always be yourself. I love you for ever.'

That's my mam. For ever, she says. Only there's no for ever, is there? Not for her, anyhow. I was supposed to keep that letter for when I was eighteen but I opened it anyway. I keep it in a box under me bed and I take it out to read from time to time – not too often, because the paper will wear out one day. It'll be like, that'll be her gone, then. I made a copy, just to remember exactly what she said, for when it gets too creased and falling to bits. I only ever read it on my own. I did it once when Tony was in the room. We share the same bedroom. I read it while he was there because I wanted him to remember my mam with me, me and him together. But he didn't want to.

'You should have kept it for later, like she asked. Anyway, you know what's in it, what's the point?' he said.

'Don't you ever miss her?' I asked him.

'Oh, f★★★ off,' he said, and he turned over and went to sleep.

See? I told you.

Anyhow. So I was picking out the tune to

7

'Cosmic Boogie' on the piano and as I did it, I was imagining how her fingers used to touch the keys and make the music come. She used to play for us all. Nan used to waltz around the room, pretending to be a ballerina. I can't play. I'd like piano lessons but I don't ask, because you know what me dad'll say?

'Billy, we can't afford enough to bloody eat, let alone ponce around on a piano, son.'

That's my dad. Him and Tony are just alike. It's all how you got to stand up for yourself and take your knocks and stick together. There's no time for remembering people, not for them. They're too busy standing up for themselves. Fighting on the picket line, I've heard them. 'Scab! Scab! Scab!' Fighting down the mine. I can just imagine them down there, fighting away at the coalface, ripping out lumps of coal like a pair of bloody mechanical diggers. And fighting each other, and fighting me too. What's the difference?

They were quarrelling again that morning.

'Come on, Dad! We'll be late! Stop faffing about!'

Tony was rushing about the place, pulling on his boots, slapping his hands together. But Dad wanted to make the place look pretty. He's always worrying about Nan being on her own in the house.

'I've time to do your nan's breakfast, haven't I?'

'For f***'s sake! Billy can do it. Come on!'

'Hang on.' Dad ran out into the yard. Tony

8

walked up and down, clucking to himself. I just sat there and picked out the tune. It's like this all the time. Quarrelling and fighting. It's all they ever do.

Dad came back in with the coal scuttle. 'There's not much of this coal left.'

'We'll be digging it out of the ground again next month.'

Dad stood there with his mouth pulled down. 'Don't kid yourself,' he said.

Tony looked at him like he was made of poison or something. You could feel the air freeze. Tony hates that sort of talk. 'You'd just pack it in and stay in bed if it wasn't for me, wouldn't you?' he said.

'Tony,' Dad began, but Tony was off.

'Suit your bloody self, I'm not waiting for youse.' He grabbed an armful of placards and made for the door.

'Tony! Tony, wait for us!' yelled Dad. But Tony was gone.

Dad didn't chase him. He just stood there. Tony reckons he's had it. He reckons he's given in. I dunno, maybe he's right.

I carried on with me tune.

'Shut it up, Billy, will you!' he yelled at me suddenly.

I took no notice. 'Mam would have let us,' I told him, picking away. He came up behind me and slammed the lid down. He only just missed my fingers. Then he ran out the door after Tony.

What's he want to stop me playing for, when he's not even here?

'I'll see you later at the Social,' he said on the way out.

Bugger! I thought. I hate it when he comes to watch me box.

'Listen. I boxed. Me dad boxed. You box.'

That's me dad. What he did two hundred years ago is what his dad did two hundred years before that and it's what I'll be doing two hundred years from now. That's how come my dad knows what's what. My brother used to take the piss out of him when he was younger.

'Yer can't tell me – Ah know!' he'd say. That was in the old days, before he turned into me dad as well. Now he's just as bad. And that's why every Saturday morning I put the gloves around me neck and I go down the club to punch someone's head in for them.

I could get into the boxing if they let me be. The thing is, I have my own ideas about it, and they don't like that. The thing about boxing, see, it's not what you do with your hands. It's what you do with your feet. George the trainer and dad, they don't understand that. They think it's just a question of how hard you hit someone in the head, but that's wrong. Look at Muhammad Ali. You can't hit him, he's not there. 'Float like a butterfly, sting like a bee.' If George had to sing that, it'd be more like 'Stand still as a bloody rock, punch like a bloody lorry.' He's always yelling at me and telling me to stop dancing about the place.

He hates it. 'Hit him! Hit him! Stand still and fight!' he yells at me. Stand still and get hit, he means. He thinks I only do it to annoy him. Once he actually climbed in the ring and held me still so the other bloke could hit me properly.

If they let me alone until I wore out the other blokes and got 'em tired in the legs, then I'd start belting 'em. But they can't wait that long. They don't think. It's tactics, see. They don't bloody think.

JACKIE ELLIOT

Well, I worry for the boy. There's no one to look out for him since his mam died. I do what I can for him, but a boy needs a mother. Especially a boy like that.

Look at this fight we're in now. It's a fight for our future, for our community. It's a fight for my job and for Tony's job – but is it a fight for Billy? See our Billy a quarter of a mile underground hacking the coal out, the sweat running black, in your eyes, down your back. That's not our Billy. All I could ever do for him was pay his way and I can't even do that now.

And I'm not sure I ever will again.

Tony thinks I'm going soft. We're owed. That's how Tony sees it. Aye, well, he's right but so what? Being owed never won owt. I remember my dad on strike in the thirties. They weren't owed then – they had power. The coal they dug ran the factories, lit the streets and the houses, drove the ships across the water. Without coal the whole bloody country dragged to a halt. Look at it now – natural gas, oil, nuclear energy. You don't have to go and dig oil and gas out of the ground with your bare hands, you just tap down into it and it shoots up like a bloody fountain. Nice and easy. And cheap.

And then, of course, there's the luxurious lifestyles folk like us insist on. Gold bath taps. Caviar with every meal. That's why it's cheaper to float coal over from Argentina than it is to pay us to dig it up out of the ground.

I don't think.

Well, I'll tell you what. If Thatcher came here today and said to me, Look, we're going to close down the mines and we're going to open up a whole bloody great town full of shiny new factories . . . I don't know rightly if I'd say yea or nay, but at least it'd be some sort of hope. Not like this. Not like, you lot aren't cost-effective, so sod off. That's Thatcher. She must have a fist where her heart is. The whole bloody community is going to be left to rot. She just doesn't care. She doesn't care about us – that goes without saying – but she doesn't care about anything else either. She doesn't care if the whole bloody country gets closed down, so long as she runs it her way. She's already shut down half of it. The mills all gone, half our industry closed down or sold off abroad. Now it's our turn. At first I thought we could do it. I thought we could teach her a lesson the other workers couldn't. Now I'm not so sure.

Well. Maybe Tony's right. Maybe I'm just going soft. I've seen it before – old blokes like me with too much to lose who've lost too much already. And me, I've already lost just about everything. My lovely Sarah gone, gone from me for ever. Every day I wake up and I think, Can she really be dead? How could that happen? It's unbelievable to me. And yet somehow, you know, here I am out of work and time on my hands, but I never seem to have a chance to even think about her. I've got my boys to bring up on my own. I've got the strike. You understand me. It's hard, it's very, very hard. I keep at it for Tony's sake because . . . well, what is there for Tony if we lose this? After all, if the world stopped tomorrow, I'd have been in love and I'd've worked and lived and had my kids. But Tony? What's he got? He was brought up to be a miner, and what's a miner without a mine?

So here I am. Fighting for Tony, even though I don't know if we can win. Fighting for Billy, even though I've got nothing for him even if we do win. I've got nowt else for them. No job. No mother. No future. Just me, here and now. It's all I've got left.

I go down every Saturday I can to watch Billy box. I miss the beginning because of the picket, but it puts you in the right frame for boxing. It gets bloody rough out there. The police, don't tell me they don't have orders, they don't need to be gentle but they don't have to be that rough. Mind, I'll tell you this, if we ever get our hands on the

14

men in those coaches going through that line, we'll tear the bastards limb from bloody limb. Some of the young lads like Tony, they want blood. They chant it sometimes. 'BLOOD BLOOD BLOOD!' Imagine sitting in that coach listening to that. And then knowing you're going to meet us at the shops or on the street or wherever the next day . . .

I don't agree with violence. That's not going to get us anywhere, there'll always be scabs – but I can understand it. Rows and rows of men, going without, putting their community and the future before their own families – and there's those bastards riding in behind a police guard to try and bring us down. Scabs. When you see men you've worked next to, men you thought were your friends – men you went to school with, or your son went to school with, people you thought you could trust – and there they are riding in behind a police guard five men thick! Well. It makes you want to kick their bloody heads in. As if it wasn't enough having to fight the bosses. To have to fight your own an' all!

So – I went in that day ready to see my boy dish out some stick. I remember the feeling when your glove connects – tok! – it goes right up your arm and into your shoulder. It's something I did, and me dad did, it's something Tony did too. Now it's Billy's turn. I keep telling him, 'You've got to be able to fight, lad. If you can't fight you can't stand

15

up for yourself, and if you can't stand up for your-self . . . well, what's the point?'

They were using the downstairs as a soup kitchen for the strikers, and so the ballet class was in the hall as well. Rows of little girls in pink going up and down, up and down.

'Bottoms out!' called the woman doing the class. I thought. Bloody hell! Ballet and boxing, what a mixture! It made me chuckle while I sat down. Ballet and boxing! They ought to put the little girls in gloves and put the lads in those poncy pink shoes they wear. That'd be a laugh!

Our Billy was in the ring.

'Go on, Billy!' I shouted. I could see the little girls turning to look at me. I nodded at our lad. I thought, Let them have a look at him, see what he can do. I hadn't been for a while. He didn't use to be much good, but he's improved lately, he's been telling me. Says his footwork's improved and his punching's coming on. 'Footwork,' I said, 'aye, you need to have footwork, just make sure you whack him one in between steps.'

Old George was checking the gloves, getting them ready.

'Go on, lads, fight fair. Give it all you got!'

The other lad was a big chubby bloke. He was taller and stronger than our Billy, but he was a bit of a porker. Footwork, I thought – Billy'll leave him standing!

Then out he came. And I thought . . . Oh, Christ!

16

I mean. What was he playing at? Muhammad Ali? More like bloody Fred Astaire. Jumping and twisting and twatting about. He was even twirling round in circles and giving his back to his opponent.

'Oh, not this again,' George groaned. 'This is man-to-man combat, not a bloody tea party. Hit him! Hit him! For god's sake . . .' He looked over to me. All I could do was shake my head.

Billy was prancing about, occasionally going up close and doing a little jab. The other bloke was just standing there hiding behind his gloves, watching.

'He's just pissing about, Greavesy,' said George. 'Hit him one. Get stuck in. He's like a fanny in a fit.'

'Watch him, Billy!' I yelled. Too late. Whack! Greavesy walked right up and smacked him one. Bang! And there was Billy on his back.

'Jesus Christ!' George was furious, absolutely furious. I suppose he felt he was letting me down as much as anything, but it's not his fault. The boy's unteachable. All that stuff about footwork! I might have known he was just daydreaming again.

'Billy Elliot, you're a disgrace to them gloves, your father and the traditions of this hall. You owe us fifty pence.'

I couldn't look any more. All I wanted to do was come along and give him some support, and what happens? I have to watch him get humiliated. I was so angry. What could I do for that boy? What had I got for him? If he can't even bloody look after himself against a fat prat like that, what is he? Eh? What is he? And what does that make me?

BILLY

'Go on – hit it. Where's your sense of rhythm? Bang bang bang! You'll stay here until you do it properly, Billy Elliot.'

Bang bloody bloody bang bang bang! How dare he! I was so angry I couldn't see straight. In front of my Dad! How bloody dare he! He knew exactly what he was doing.

'You're a disgrace to them gloves, your father and blah blah blah . . .' Bastard! I tried to imagine the punchbag was his face but I was so cross I was just swinging and swiping and missing the sodding thing.

'I'm going to glue your bloody feet to the ground, Elliot! I'm going to stop you pratting about if it's the last thing I do. Go on . . . hit it!'

Bloody bloody . . . bang bang bang! How dare he? F★★★ him!

'Bottoms in. Feel the music. And – one and two and three and four. And five and six. Lift your arms. Feel the music! Susan! Drop that hip.'

Down the hall that woman was doing her ballet class. There was some old bloke on the piano.

Plinkity plonk, plinkity plink. One and two and three and four . . .

I began hitting more slowly, in time to the music. It made me snigger. I reckon if old George'd guessed I was beating up the punchbag in time to poncy ballet music, he'd have blown himself to bits. It worked, though. That bag was getting it.

'And one and two and three and four and five and six . . .'

'That's better. Why don't you do that to someone's head one day?' George fished out a bunch of keys from his pocket and chucked them to me.

'Give them to Mrs Wilkinson when you've finished. I'll see you next week.'

Out he went. Good riddance to bad rubbish, I thought. I focused on the bag and pretended it was his head. Beat the fat bastard up by ballet!

'One and two . . .' And bang and thump. 'Three and four.' And whack and bump. Bang bang bang. I wondered if Muhammad Ali did workouts to music. It wouldn't surprise me. The trouble with George is, he's teaching boxing like it used to be, not like how it is. Same as everything else round here – about sixty years out of date.

Not that I give a toss about boxing, anyhow. Michael's right. You'd never get him down here whacking away at bags of leather.

'F***ing stupid. Kicking people's heads in. What for? It's a load of old shite. I don't know why you bother.'

'You got to look after yourself, haven't you?'

'I'd rather f***ing run away.'

'That won't get you very far.'

'Well, how far do you think you're going to go? Look at them gloves, man, they went out with the Ark.'

'These are me dad's.'

'Exactly.'

Bloody Michael. One thing though. He's always himself, like me mam says. God knows what that is, though.

The music changed pace.

'And hold. Support yourselves. Don't look at me, Susan, look ahead, where's your confidence? Come on. And . . . down. Lovely. Good. Eyes front, Debbie. And five and six and . . . For god's sake, stop quivering, girl! And three and four and five and six and seven and eight. Thank you, Mr Braithwaite. Right, into the centre, girls, please.'

I took the gloves off, hung them round me neck and went over to have a look.

They looked pretty, the girls, in their pink tights and little dresses and things. Old George had told us, no hanky-panky with the ballet lesson happening right next to us. Some of the lads had been calling out – you know, 'Fwoar, never mind bottoms in – tits out!' and all that. Not that many

21

of them girls had tits yet, mind, but the way them girls bend over and lift their legs right up – Dave Michael said it'd be nice if they left their knickers off. What a view! He said you'd be able to see halfway to China. He's filthy. He gets it off his dad. Look at them! If they were prancing around like that any other way their mams'd be onto them, we'd all be calling them little sluts, but because it's the ballet they can flash their fannies and no one cares. Tell you the truth, I felt a bit rude watching them, like a dirty old man. You know?

'Miss, the keys . . . the keys, miss!'

She just ignored me.

'Not now, three, four. And five, and six . . .'

She didn't seem to mind us watching, though.

'Right, Mr Braithwaite. "The Sun'll Come Out Tomorrow". Fat chance. And . . . port de bras forward and up.'

The music started up again and the girls stepped up all together. It was pretty clever, really. All in step, lifting up their arms, twirling round. Step and two, and down and two, and round and two. It was interesting, really. Pretty easy, though. I reckoned anyone could do it if they wanted. I didn't know why them lasses had to spend so much time doing something as obvious as that, like. That pointy bit with the toes. I stretched mine out to see. See? Easy!

'Why don't you have a go?'

It was Debbie Wilkinson. She's in the same year as me at school.

'Nah,' I said. Imagine it! Me doing ballet!

'It's not as easy as it looks,' she said.

'Get off,' I said.

'Port de bras forward and up. And . . . hold!'

They all froze in mid-air like. I held me breath. It really looked pretty good. I stuck me leg out like them. Easy. Mrs Wilkinson went around among them, straightening legs and things.

'And up!'

They all stood up straight. 'I bet you couldn't do it,' said Debbie.

'Anyone could do that.'

She put her leg out with her toes pointed. 'Do that,' she said.

I stuck it out just to show her.

'There you are. See?' she said. It was true, hers was much more pointy than mine.

'Well, I've got me boots on.'

'Anyhow, it's shaking like a leaf,' she teased me. I looked down. It was. She did hers again and, all right, it was stiller than mine. Quite a bit stiller, even though it was shaking a bit at the toe.

'OK, girls. To the barre. Thank you, Mr Braithwaite.' Mrs Wilkinson walked past the pianist, pinched a fag from his pocket and lit it without a missing a beat. 'And one and two and three and four.'

My nan's always saying how she could have been

a professional dancer. She reckoned Mam could have been too, but dancing wasn't her thing. Nan used to take her to do the ballet when she was a girl, but Mam never took to it like she did. She was a musician, Nan said. She loved to play. I thought of Nan doing all those movements with her arms up, and Mam doing the same thing. See? There's things in our family other than boxing.

The girls were all at the other end of the barre, so I had a little go behind Miss's. Bend and stretch and legs out! I bent and stuck me leg out and peeked at it over my shoulder.

Debbie was right. It wasn't as easy as it looked.

I was trying to follow what they were doing, and it really was pretty difficult. The thing was, I found out, to let the music do it for you. You know? It wasn't like Marc Bolan or Bowie but it had a good rhythm. You had to get into it. You had to feel the music, like Miss kept saying. And then . . . up and down and one and two and three and four and . . .

'. . . boots off!'

'Ow!'

She was treading on my foot. A whiff of fag smoke drifted past my face. It made me cough.

'What size are you? Two, three. Boots off! Four, five. And six and seven.'

'Miss, what about the keys?'

'And eight and nine and ten.' She was off again, wandering around among the girls. I don't know why she wanted me to take me boots off, but I did as I was told. Maybe you weren't allowed near the barre or something with your boots on. I was doing the second laces when she dropped something in front of me.

Bloody great pair of ballet shoes.

'I dare you,' she said. 'Prepare. You can't get a decent line with those boots.'

Well. There was no one about to see, just the girls. And you know what? I reckon they liked it, having a lad in with them. I reckon they thought I was something a bit different. Why not? Just to show them.

She was a good teacher, that Mrs Wilkinson. I didn't hardly have time to think about how stupid I looked. She had me going up and down, up and down. One and two and three and four and five. And I reckon she thought I was pretty good at it, an' all, because when she made us all hold with our arms stretched out in front and our legs stretched out behind us, she came and checked me over.

'Nice straight leg,' she said. See, it's easier if you wear the proper shoes, you can't get a decent line with those boots on. 'Good arch,' she said, whatever that is. It was bloody hard, though. You try it – just stand there on one leg, with your other leg out behind and your arms out in front and just stand there for a minute or two without shaking. You'll see. It's hard. You have to be bloody strong.

25

'Turn that leg out. Drop that hip.'

She didn't say much. She never said anything. I just had the impression she thought I was doing all right, somehow.

Afterwards, when I was walking home, she pulled up alongside me in her car. The window came down. She had that Debbie in the back of her car, too. I'd never realised she was her daughter.

She breathed out a load of smoke through the window. 'You owe me fifty pence,' she said.

'No, I don't.'

'You do. Bring it along next week.'

'I have to do boxing, miss.'

'But you're crap at boxing,' said Debbie. The little cow must've been watching me.

'I'm not,' I said. 'He just caught me, that's all.'

'Shut up, Debbie.' Mrs Wilkinson looked back at me. 'Thought you enjoyed it.'

I said nowt.

'Please yourself, darling,' she told me, and she drove off. I could see Debbie's funny face peering at me out the back window as they went.

She was right, though – I did enjoy it. The music was a bit dull, that's all. I reckon I could have really got into it if she had something better than that old fart on the piano. T. Rex or Bowie. Pan's People. Or Fred Astaire. He can dance! My nan likes Fred Astaire, we had one of his films on the telly the other day. If I was going to be a dancer, that's the sort of thing it'd have to be. You know, 'High hat'?

High hat! I ran and spun and jumped as I ran down the road, and the thought of the music filled me up till it ran squeaking and shouting and spinning out of my ears.

Next day I was aching all over.

That ballet, it's bloody addictive, you know. I was thinking about it all the next week. One and two and up and down. I kept hearing her voice going on at me. When you put your arms and legs into those positions, it's like a note of music. You hold it in the air . . . and then, whoosh! It goes off into the rest of the tune.

Aye, interesting. The only thing with it is, it makes me feel like a right sissy. I mean! Ponce, two, three, twat, two, three and prat about and four and five and six and shite shite shite.

Nah. Imagine what me Dad'd say! Or Tony! They'd go barmy! I mean, what good's ballet down a mine? Only problem with that is, what mine? The union leader Arthur Scargill says they have a secret plan to close all the mines down, so if he's right I might as well be dancing as owt, because there won't be any mines left for me to go down by the time I'm old enough. On the news they say the miners'll be back at work in a few more weeks. Once winter comes. Starved out. Aye, well, we're not starving yet. It's been a long time since we had a joint of meat on Sunday, that's all.

There's no one to cook it anyhow. Tony has a go but he's not as good as our mam was.

Not everyone thinks ballet's crap. Some of them lasses at school said it's dead brave of me to do a ballet class. Aye, and some of 'em told the other lads what I was up to. I had Dave Sullivan and that crowd on at me in the playground the other day.

'Eh, Billy, give us a turn. Show yer fanny, will you?' But I don't care about them. What do they know? I'm used to being picked on. That Debbie's latched onto me an' all, which doesn't help either. I reckon her mam wants me to go so's she can get more customers. If the boys started ballet there'd be twice as many takers, wouldn't there? Not that she's short of a bob or two, I reckon, with her posh voice and all. Bloody middle-class Millie, that's what she is. Not like us. Not like mining. Try her down a mine! It'd bloody kill her!

Debbie was on at me on the way home from school the other day.

'Plenty of boys do ballet, you know,' she said.

'Do they f***. What boys?'

'Nobody round here, but plenty do.'

'Poofs,' I told her.

'Not necessarily,' she said.

We got to the top of the hill and looked down. You could see the mine from there. All around it were rings and rings and rings of miners and coppers. They had their shields shining in the sun.

There were some of them on horseback. One of the shifts was coming out.

'That Wayne Sleep. He's not a poof,' she said.

'Sounds pretty poofy to me,' I told her. Down below there was a noise like drums. I peered down. The coppers were beating their shields with their batons.

'It's like Zulu, isn't it?' said Debbie.

'Aye, like Zulu.' There were bloody thousands of them and they were still coming. You could see more vans coming down the hills, like lions gathering. Or vultures. One drove past us. I could see the faces of the policemen inside staring out at us.

'He's as fit as an athlete.'

'What?'

'That Wayne Sleep. He's as fit as an athlete.'

'I bet he couldn't beat Daley Thompson.'

'Maybe not in a race, but in stamina. Why don't you come next time? You could just watch.'

'I gotta go boxing, haven't I?'

'Please yourself.' She turned off to go. She lived on the other side of the village. Big houses, gardens. Middle-class Millie. 'See you, then.'

'Aye. See you. Ta-ra.'

Debbie walked off up the hill. I stared down at the mine. The miners on the picket line started hooting at the policemen banging their shields, as if they were monkeys. What a racket! It was a war all right, but you know what? They looked like a bloody chorus line in a Fred Astaire movie.

I bet I could have made a great film director if I was given the chance. I bet no one else would think of using all those policemen in a chorus line. I began to tap my foot and sing . . . 'High hat'.

I was so busy watching, I didn't hear the cop car come up behind me until it gave a little poop. I nearly jumped out of me skin. The copper driving smiled at me and winked. I walked out of the road and watched them drive off. Out of the back window, the coppers waved me goodbye. I just ignored them.

That Debbie gives me the shivers sometimes, actually. She's a funny little dried-up-looking thing. Middle-class. You'd expect her to want me to fanny about doing ballet, but she wasn't the only one. Michael thought it was all right, too. Mind you, Michael's . . . well, Michael's Michael, isn't he? He's a good friend, though, he never tries to tell you what you should be doing. I was showing him some of the moves under Gat's Cope when we were doing cross-country at school. Him and me, we don't like cross-country. Actually, Michael hates all sports. I like some of it. I used to spend ages learning tricks at football. You know the sort of thing – like grabbing the ball between your ankles and flipping it up over your head. Then, if you're fast enough, you can spin round and slam it one, right in the back of the net. Only it never works like that on the pitch. I spent ages learning that one. Or tapping the ball from one toe to the other, up in the air in little skips, then knocking it between your opponent's legs and running off behind him. I've done that one a few times in a real game.

The ballet's the same in some ways. You have to spend ages learning how to do the moves just right. It's only, there's no ball involved.

Anyhow, while the others go running round a dirty great long loop from the end of the school playing field and right round Gat's Wood and back, me and Michael hang around the back and slip down into the old tunnel under the track. Then we sit around chatting for ten minutes until the others come along over the bridge. Once they've run round the corner, we come back up and follow behind them – last every time, but who cares?

I showed him some of the moves in the tunnel. 'Put your leg like that,' I said. I had to straighten it up for him. 'Arm out, one, two!' He looked over his shoulder and grinned at me.

'Eyes forward,' I told him. I showed him all the moves, and you know what? He wasn't anywhere near as good at it as I was. I had to show him how.

'You've had lessons,' he complained.

'Lesson. Just one,' I told him.

'Are you going back?'

'Nah. What for?'

'You're good at it, aren't you?'

'I reckon.'

'Well, then.'

'I feel like a right idiot.'

'You are a right idiot. So what's the difference?' He paused and looked at me. 'I think you look nice, actually. I think you should do it. It looks very . . .'

'What?'

'Well, not tough, but . . . manly.'

'Manly? What sort of a word's that? Anyhow, it's for girls.'

'It's different when men do it. It's like the gymnastics on the telly. The men are different, aren't they? They're so much stronger, like. Graceful but strong. You know what I mean?' He comes out with it sometimes, Michael. Manly! But I knew what he meant. Gymnastics is a good way of looking at it. The ballet's like that. I could jump higher than those girls. If you get your muscles underneath the jump, you go up like a f***ing bird.

So in the end I did have another go at it, after all. I thought, Just once. When I left the house I had no intention of doing it. Dad and Tony had their usual quarrel and went off to the picket line. I took my fifty pence off the fridge, got the gloves and off I went. But once I got into the changing rooms and I heard George going on, bang bang bang . . . oh, my heart sank. I thought, Banging about in the ring and getting twatted by some dopey piece of shite – not for me, thanks. Michael

32

was right, it's stupid. So I hid in one of the cubicles in the changing room, waited until they'd all gone, and then sneaked down to the ballet class. It was downstairs this time so no one would ever know I'd been. It was just curiosity. I didn't care that much. I just wanted to see how good I was at it, really. And I quite liked the girls all looking at me as well. And I didn't half mind looking at them, either!

It started off boring and embarrassing. They were doing all these moves one after the other and I had no idea what was coming next. I was going one way and they were going the other. How was I supposed to know what to do? They'd been doing it for ages. I bet I could have done any of those moves better than they could, but I didn't know which one was coming next.

Miss was going, 'One two three, one two three, one two three,' but how can you stay in rhythm if you don't know what's coming next? I had no idea what I was doing. I just stopped.

'What's this?' she said.

'I don't know what to do, miss.'

'Follow the others. Go to the back so you can watch – two three, one two three. Where's those arms, two three, one two three.'

I did me best, but I dunno. I was thinking, I've had enough of this. I was thinking it was more fun getting your head kicked in than being a prat here. But then she showed me the spin.

I'd seen them before on TV. You know,

someone spins round and round dead fast and then stops – comes suddenly to a dead stand-still in exactly the same position as when they started off. It's pretty spectacular, really. If you did that in a boxing ring, no one would know what was going on. You'd spin round really fast, and you'd come out of it with a punch – man, you'd knock your opponent flying! Anyway, it's like all these things – there's a trick to it, see. I never realised. You have to find a spot on the wall, stare at it, get your arms right – the balance is in the arms, see – then push off into your spin, really, really fast – and then stop so you're staring at exactly the same point. It has to be exactly the same spot, mind – it's not good starting off staring at a picture on the wall and end up looking at the lampshade. If you get it right, you go like a top. If you get it wrong, you end up on your back.

Anyhow, I was crap at that too. She showed us it over and over. Some of the girls did it pretty well, really. I tried to imitate them, but she wasn't having it.

'Come on, Billy, you're not a girl, are you? Put some strength into it! Spin it, spin it! You're a man. You've got to go off like a rocket!'

So I did. I span round so fast me feet slipped and I ended up sprawled out on the floor like a prat. The girls stared down at me. They didn't dare laugh, though. She came down on anyone who laughed. You have to be prepared to be a bit of a prat when you start off learning these things, so you can end up good. Same as anything.

'Practise at home,' she said. And then we went to barre, which was a lot better because it was all slow and you could see the moves easily and I could do that OK.

At the end of it I was knackered, but I felt great. That spin – I knew I could do it. It was just a question of practice. I was sitting on a bench pulling me jumper on and that Debbie was hanging around me again, watching like I was a TV set or something.

'See,' she said. 'I said it was harder than it looks, didn't I?'

'Aye, you did.'

'The spin's hard, isn't it?' She practised it a couple of times.

'You're not as fast as me,' I told her.

'You can't even do it,' she scoffed.

I got up to show her. I did a slow one to start with and it wasn't half bad, but when I did it fast it was no good. I couldn't keep me balance.

'You need to go round at least twice. A strong lad like you.' It was Mrs Wilkinson.

'Aye.' I sat down and started packing my bag. She nodded at Debbie.

'Scram.'

'Why, Mam?'

'What did you call me?'

'Miss. Sorry.'

'Go on.'

Debbie cleared off and Miss looked down at me, holding her fag to her mouth and squinting through the smoke.

'So then. Do we get the pleasure of your company next week?'

'Dunno. It's just . . . I feel like a right sissy.'

'Then don't act like one. Fifty pence.'

I handed over the money. She pointed at my ballet shoes.

'Well, if you're not coming, give us your shoes back.'

I hesitated. Ballet – well, I didn't care for it all that much, but I wanted to learn how to do that spin. I wanted to do it in the boxing ring. That'd show 'em!

'Nah, you're all right,' I said.

'Right,' she said, and she turned on her heel without even saying goodbye or anything, and walked straight out.

And you know what? I didn't realise how much I liked it until I found myself dancing all the way home. I felt really light-headed. I went skittering and jumping all the way, and it wasn't till I was standing in the kitchen with the ballet shoes in one hand and the boxing gloves around me neck that I thought, What have I done? What was I going to do with them shoes? If Dad caught me with them he'd bloody kill me.

Nan was there waiting for me.

'Ooh, ballet shoes,' she said, her little old face

all lighting up. 'I used to dance. I could have been a professional.'

'Don't tell, Nan, will you?' I begged – although it wouldn't make any difference. No one takes any notice of what she says. I ran upstairs and lifted the mattress off to stuff them under there, but I was only halfway through when Dad came in. Shit! I never knew he was at home. I stuffed the ballet shoes under me just in time.

'What are you doing, crawling about like creeping Jesus?'

'Nowt.'

'Where've you been anyway? We found your nan round at the Spar.'

'Boxing, where'd you think?'

He stared down at me. I was lying on the bed keeping the shoes hidden under me, trying to look normal like.

'What are you doing?' he demanded.

'I forgot me gloves. I thought they might be under the bed.' I peered down over the edge of the bed as if I was looking underneath it.

He looked at me, then at the floor, then back at me. Then he pointed to the gloves lying there next to the bed.

'What's them, then?'

'Oh. Right.'

He stood there looking at me – waiting for me to move, I expect, but I couldn't. I felt like a prat.

'You watch out for them gloves, they were me dad's.'

'I know.'

'Right.' He walked out. That was a close call! If my dad ever catches me doing ballet, he'll bloody kill me. I won't do it for long, though. Just for a bit. Just until I get that spin right. Then I'll go down the boxing hall and shoot someone's head right off!

JACKIE ELLIOT

I knew there was something funny going on. Billy is my son and I stand by him till the day I die, but. Put it like this: he's a bit of an individualist, Billy. He's always got these weird things he's trying to do. It used to be balancing a stick on the end of his nose. He was only eight or so. Then there was the cardboard box. He used to sit in it singing to himself. That's just kids, you might say, but Billy was ten. I'd not be seen dead in a cardboard box when I was ten. It was when his mother was ill, so perhaps that's understandable. But what about the neck-twisting? That went on for ages. He'd turn round and look behind him, twisting his neck round as far as he could, over and over again. He said it was just a habit, but what sort of a habit is that? It's not like picking your nose or biting your nails. Once I took him to the cinema and he spent the whole time twisting round in his seat. He was just stretching the muscles in his neck but the woman behind didn't know that, she thought he was staring at her. It was so embarrassing. You can't stop him. He can't stop himself.

'Your son's staring at me,' she said.

'Aye, and I paid good money for this film,' I told her back.

It was football for a while, that was OK. He used to go out into the street and practise flipping the ball over his head with his feet, or keepsie-upsies or something like that. He was never all that good on the pitch, mind, but at least it was good healthy practice, the sort of thing you'd expect for a kid of his age.

Now it was spinning round in circles.

He denied it at first, but I kept catching him at it. In the kitchen, in the hall, in the yard, in his bedroom. All the bloody time. Staring into space like an idiot, holding out his arms and then hurling himself round in a bloody great spin and falling over, half the time. I sent him out to make tea once, and when he didn't come back for ages I went to have a look. There he was, staring away, just about to go off.

'Billy,' I said, just as he let himself off, and he went spinning round, trying to look over his shoulder at the same time, and he went crashing into the table and sent the lot flying – milk every-where, sugar upside down, mugs broken.

Tony came rushing in from the hall. 'What are you doing, man?'

'I'm just practising a spin. It's a boxing move,' he said.

'It's not like any boxing move I've ever seen,' I told him. Boxing move! It was another one of his stupid habits.

'Now don't start doing that all the time,' I warned him. 'You'll wreck the bloody house doing that.'

'Aye, and who's going to pay for those mugs and all? You've got no bloody sense,' goes Tony.

'All right, Dad, all right.' But of course he didn't stop. He can't help himself once he gets going. He's like a bloody rabbit with the eyes too big or something. At least he started doing it outside after that. He was pretending to do boxing practice, but was he heck. I crept out into the yard to have a look and there he was, same old thing. Arms curved out to one side, then he flung 'em round and went hurtling round in a circle. The weird thing was the way he was staring into space. And the gloves – aye, he had the gloves on. He looked like a bloody madman. He scares me sometimes, our Billy. I don't know what to make of him.

I went out and had a word with him.

'What are you doing, son? You look like you're having a fit or something.'

'I'm practising, Dad.'

'No, you're not practising. Practising what? Looking like a fanny? Don't you care what people think of you?'

'It's just a bloody spin.'

'Well, don't do it. Not out here where people can see.'

'But you told me not to do it in the house!'

'Just don't do it, that's all. OK?'

41

I didn't see it so much after that, but I knew he was still at it. I could hear him falling about all over. Banging on the landing, crashing about in the kitchen. I was forever yelling, 'Stop bloody banging!' He fell in the bath doing it one time. It was his Sunday-night bath, there was this almighty splash and when I went up, there he was, staring at himself in the mirror, fully dressed, soaking wet, arms out ready to have another go.

'You're doing that again!' I told him.

'I fell in the bath, that's all,' he said.

I didn't bother saying any more. I just rolled my eyes and left him to it.

He had me worried then. I had a word with Susan Harris down the road, but she reckoned I should take no notice.

'He's just a lad, he's only twelve, he's still a baby really,' she said. 'Let him be, Jackie, he'll be all right. He needs to let off steam somehow.'

She's brought up four of her own, Susan, so I thought she knew best. I suppose it's not the sort of thing your dad lets you do, but maybe your mam'd turn a blind eye.

I'll give him this, though, our Billy, he did it. Whatever it was he was trying to do, he did it. I was coming back home from the shops with a pint of milk in me pocket and there he was in the yard doing his stuff. I stood and watched. Bolt upright, staring at the wall, arms out – bang, round he went two or three times, I couldn't count, he was going so fast. And then came to stop like a slammed door, bang.

'Yes!' He was so made up, I couldn't help smiling. 'Yes, yes, I did it, I did it, I did it!' He went dancing around the yard stamping and whooping. I never saw a kid so happy.

'Yer did it then,' I said, and he nearly fell over. He'd been so concentrated he never noticed me.

'Ow, god. Dad! Ah! You scared me.'

'Aye. So you've done it, then, have you?'

'Watch!' And he had another go, but he couldn't do it this time, not with me watching. He was all over the place.

'I did it just then, though. Did you see me?'

'Yeah. Pretty good stuff. So have you tried it down the boxing club yet, then?'

'No, not yet.'

'Are you going to?'

'Soon as I've got it right each time.' He was already standing there having another go.

'So, is this something George taught you, now, Billy?'

'George? No. I made it up myself.'

'Did you now? And what does he think about it?'

Billy looked sideways at me and grinned. 'He doesn't mind. He just lets me get on with it.'

'Right. Well, you'll have a surprise for him next Saturday then, won't you?'

Jesus. Poor old George'll have a heart attack. Well, I didn't have the heart to ask Billy how it went, I knew what'd happen. He'd get away with it a couple of times, and then someone would come up and whack him while he was spinning round defenceless. He was going round so fast, all you'd have to do was hold your glove out and he'd knock his own block off for you. It'd be like putting a stick into the wheels of a bike as it went downhill.

He didn't care, though. He was gone. It was jumps next. He started doing these poncy jumps – big jumps, mind, right high, big, long jumps, but with his arms up over his head like a bloody ballet dancer. It was beginning to drive me barmy. The spinning was bad enough, but he looked like such a prat doing this. And the noise he made jumping up and down – it went through the whole house. Bang, crash, wallop! Christ!

'Is this another boxing move, then?' I asked him.

'Aye.'

'So did you try the spin, then?'

'Aye.'

'Did it work?'

'Not really.'

'Right. Look.' I decided to give him a hand. He was just going to get himself into a mess like this. George had obviously decided to let him fanny around on his own. 'Look, son, you've got to keep your hands up at all times, even when you're leaping. Keep your guard up!' I put his gloves up round his chin. 'Do a jump like that.'

'I can't, Dad, it's balance, you have to be

balanced, you see.' Then he started to show me how he had to have his arms in the right place so he could leap properly. He had it all thought out, aye, a whole bloody philosophy of pratting about. I gave up in the end. What's the point? Maybe George was right, maybe all you could do was let him do his own thing and wait for some common sense to work its way into that thick head of his all on its own. Maybe if he got knocked down enough times, he'd start trying to fight back. I wouldn't count on it myself. The only thing was the bloody fifty pences. I had to scrape and save for that money. I was paying for him to learn how to defend himself, not to prance about like a bloody girl.

I suppose George knows what he's doing. I've stopped going down meself, after what happened last time. I've enough on my plate as it is without trying to turn our Billy into something you'd recognise. Tony, for instance. He scares me worse than Billy, he's getting so wild. I'm scared the lad's going to do something stupid.

The strike's been going on for four months now with no end in sight. I've used up all me savings. I've never been so poor. Well, it's getting us all down, isn't it, but it's worst for the young ones. I see my mates on the line and down the club and . . . well, no one says anything. You can't say anything, you can't let the side down. But I reckon I'm not the only one who thinks the same.

We've had it this time. Things have changed.

It's not going to end soon, either. Not this week or next week or next month. Maybe not even this year. But some time, sooner or later. It's just a question of how much we suffer in the meantime and how quickly they close us down after.

I don't blame Tony for being angry, but you don't have to be stupid about it. I can see in his face how much he'd just love to give someone something they'll remember. I've felt it myself. The only difference is, I'm not going to do it. He might. Let's face it – what's he got to lose? His job? Like hell.

We were out shopping the other day, me and him. I was asking him about our Billy – if he'd noticed anything odd about him lately.

'Odd? What do you want, a list?' he said.

'I'm worried about him.'

'He's a bloody fruitcake. If he mucks around with my records any more I'll twat him one, that's all. They're getting all scratched.'

'He's your little brother.'

'I don't care who he is. How am I going to replace them when he's finished ruining 'em for me? I'm not exactly loaded, am I?'

'I'm sorry I asked.'

He was fuming. Any little thing sets him off these days. It's not fair, though. It's not Billy's fault we're out. 'I've got enough on my plate without having to play mam to Billy.'

'He needs his mother,' I snapped.

'Aye, and who doesn't?' he snapped back.

'He's a kid. You're a working man,' I said. But I was sorry as soon as I said it. Tony doesn't mention her to me and I don't mention her to him, but he must miss her as much as anyone else. It was unfair of me to pull Sarah on him as if she was Billy's mother and not his.

'I'm sorry,' I told him. But he was already off on something else. It had just come round the aisle of the supermarket. Gary Stewart with a nice full trolley of groceries.

'Well, look at this,' says Tony.

'Careful now,' I muttered. It's only a matter of time before he lashes out, and then what? Straight into nick, that's what. They don't bother much about justice when they're dealing with us lot. They're flinging the book at any miner who gets done and you can guarantee the company won't be taking on anyone with a record at the end of it. One punch and that's it. Steve Willis got three months for kicking someone up the arse. Oh, aye, don't kid yourself. The law's a weapon, and it's not our weapon. When did working men ever have the law on their side? Lawyers, judges, police chiefs. Not exactly from working backgrounds, are they?

'All right, scab?' called Tony. You could tell Gary was a scab just by looking at his trolley. No striker gets a load of shopping like that six months into this strike. Gary had it hard, he had a lot of commitments, but who doesn't? It's this sort of thing that's the worst of it. Gary and Tony went to school together. They were mates once. Not any more.

Tony was heading over there.

'Scabs eat well,' I called out.

'Got enough food there, have you? What are you doing, eh?' Tony banged his basket against Gary's. I wanted to tell him to leave it out, but I bit me lip. He's old enough to look after himself.

'You were me best mate. First rule of the union, Gary, you know that. Never cross a picket line. We're all f***ed if you don't remember that.'

'We're already f***ed, Tony, mate.'

'I'm not your f***ing mate. And if we do lose, it'll be because of the likes of you!'

He was getting worked up. But Gary'd had enough. He pushed the trolley and let go. 'F***ing hell,' he said. 'Bollocks! So it's all my fault then. Fine!' He turned his back and walked out. I thought Tony was going to go after him but he just stood there staring.

'Shit. Pity he hadn't paid for that food, we could have had it,' he said. He picked up a bottle of wine from the top of the heap. It looked like bloody Christmas, that trolleyload.

'F*** it,' he whispered. 'F*** it!'

He's going to lump someone. I know it. I just hope it's not a bloody copper.

★   ★   ★

On the picket line, Friday morning, it gets worse. More and more pickets, more and more anger. Everyone's getting in on it. Students, commies, teachers on holiday, people from halfway round the world – and half the bloody police in Great Britain fencing us off from the scabs on their scab bus going in to do their scab labour. You wouldn't get me on that bus, not for all the money in the Bank of England. If I'm going down, I'm going down fighting.

There was eggs going over me head. Couple of bricks. Things are getting tough. I was right next to George, we had our arms linked and the whole crowd was heaving forward, and then the coppers were shoving us back, and we were heaving forward again. It was open bloody warfare.

There was a lull in between buses, George had a word with me. 'Listen, Jackie,' he says. 'If it's the fifty pence a session, forget it. I can do without it. I don't do it for the money, you know.'

'What are you on about?'

'The boxing, man. I haven't seen hide nor hair of young Billy for months, I was gonna say something but I thought it might be embarrassing.'

I was amazed. He's been away every Saturday morning.

'First I've heard about it,' I said. 'He's always at it. He never has the gloves off.' I didn't tell him about the spins and the jumping, though.

'Send him round to my house and I'll knock some sense into him,' said George. Then the police came surging forward. Someone lobbed a brick overhead – crash – right into the side of the coach.

'SCAB SCAB SCAB SCAB!' We pressed forward so hard I was lifted almost off my feet. If you fell down in the middle of this lot, you'd never get up.

If our Billy was pocketing them fifty pences, I'd bloody kill him. He knows how hard things are. I meant to say summat to him that evening, but we had a meeting at the Social and I forgot. Next morning was a Saturday and I was going to get him at breakfast before the picket, but I never had a chance. He came running downstairs stuffing something up his coat and off out the door before you could say a word.

'Oi! What about your breakfast?' yelled Tony.

'See yer!' He was off and away. I just caught sight of him disappearing round the corner as I stuck me head out of the door.

'Billy! Billy!' I yelled. But he was gone. I thought, What the hell's he up to? What's he doing now?

BILLY

I was jumping so high, I could see out of the window and right over the shed where they keep the sports gear. Miss kept saying to me, 'It's not just height, Billy. Where's your control? You're not concentrating!' Well, I was concentrating. I was concentrating on getting up high. It just made me feel so good, floating up over the heads of them little lasses. They were like little bits of fluff floating around me knees.

I could do all the plies and the jumps and font de bras and all that. Miss says I've got promise. She spends half the lesson just teaching me – she doesn't bother with the others half the time. They're always moaning on about it.

'Can we have a go, miss? When's it our turn, miss? It's not fair, miss, just because he's a boy, miss . . .'

'Shut up, Debbie, I'm busy.'

Oh, I'd got right into it. I was looking forward to the Saturday lesson all week. Once I started, I could just go on for ever. It was right what Debbie said about stamina. It may look easy, but it's not. It's hard. I'd got so fit it'd made me better at footy and running and everything. I could keep going for hours.

I must have been mad.

It had to happen. I was kidding meself. Michael kept warning me. 'He'll find out. What are you going to do then?' I knew he was right, but it was like, if I kept on doing it and not thinking about it, nothing'd happen. I kept thinking, Just this week, just one more lesson, then I'll go back to the boxing. But I got more and more into it, and better and better at it, and Dad never turned up to watch me at George's any more . . . I just thought it was going to go on for ever.

And of course, when it did happen, it wasn't just questions and getting suspicious and everything. He only bloody turned up right in the middle of class.

'Pick up your leg, Billy. Swing it! Swing two three, round two three, up two three. What do you call that? Let's have a bit of grace, Billy Elliot!'

I was swinging me leg round, slow circle, trying to make it as smooth as cream – and I looked up and there was me dad standing in the door.

Christ! I just froze in me tracks. I thought I was going to die. I thought he was going to rush out and kill me. Miss was still going on . . .

'Up two three, swing two three. Like a princess, Deborah. Beautiful necks! One two three . . . what's up with you?'

She said that when she saw me standing still.

Then the music stopped and she turned round and saw Dad. He'd gone blood red.

'You! Out! Now!' he snapped.

I could see her out of the corner of me eye, leaning forward towards him as if she could eat him for breakfast – and she would have done, and all. Well, she'd've tried anyhow, she doesn't take anything sitting down. The last thing I wanted was a screaming match between her and me dad. I started walking towards him. 'Please, miss. Don't,' I hissed as I went past. It was so embarrassing. Dad thought I was a pansy for dancing; she thought I was a pansy for not standing up to him. I'd had it.

The door banged behind me. He grabbed my arm and pushed me in front.

'Right, you've got some explaining to do,' he said. And he marched me home.

He didn't say a word all the way back. That's how he does it, he makes you sweat. All the way home, down Union Street, up the High Street, along Macefield Road. Not a word. The bastard.

Back home he pointed at a chair behind the table, staring at me all the while he was taking his coat off. Then he sat down opposite me. And he still hadn't said a word. See? The longer he goes without saying anything, the worse trouble you're in. This time I was wondering if he was every gonna speak to me again.

I knew what he wanted. He wanted to me to

say sorry. Well, I wasn't going to. He could wait for ever. It was stupid! What had I done wrong?

'Ballet,' he said at last.

'So what's wrong with ballet?' I said. Me nan was sitting on a chair by the window eating a pork pie and watching us like we were on the telly. I looked at her. It was easier than having to look at him. I could see him turning red again out of the corner of my eye.

'What's wrong with ballet? Look at me, Billy. Are you trying to wind me up?'

'It's perfectly normal,' I sad, turning to face him.

'Normal?' I was scared. He'd gone all white around the lips.

'I used to go to ballet,' said me nan.

'See?' I said.

'For your nan. For girls, Billy. Not for lads. Lads do football or boxing or wrestling or summat.'

'What lads do wrestling?' I asked, and I had him there, because no one I know does wrestling round here.

'You know what I mean.'

'I don't know what you mean.'

'Don't start, Billy.'

'I don't see what's wrong with it, that's all.'

'You know perfectly well what's wrong with it.'

'No, I don't.'

'You do.'

'No, I don't!'

'Yes, you bloody well do. Who do you think I am? You know quite nicely.'

'It's just dancing. That's all. What's wrong with that?'

The thing is . . . All right, I knew what he meant. At least, I used to know. Ballet isn't what boys do. It's not football and boxing and being hard. And it's not going on strike and standing up for yourself and sticking it out with your mates and all hanging in together. It's not mining. It's not the union. It's not what we do.

Well, maybe I'm not mining either. And even if I was, so what? Why isn't it what we do? Just because no one's ever done it before, that's all. Well, once I've done it, it is what we do, because I'm one of us too. It doesn't have to be like him or not at all. Just because I like dancing doesn't mean I'm turning into someone else.

Does it?

'You're asking for a hiding.'

'No, I'm not. Honest, Dad, I'm not!' As far as he was concerned I was just being stubborn, but I really didn't understand why it was so bloody important that I shouldn't do ballet.

'You are, Billy!'

'It's not just poofs, Dad. Some ballet dancers are as fit as athletes. It's hard work. What about Wayne Sleep?'

'Wayne Sleep?'

I wish I hadn't said that. Wayne. Even as I said it I remembered how it sounded when Debbie first said the name to me. Wayne Sleep? Poof! That's what it sounded like.

But now he'd had enough. 'Listen, son, from now on you can forget about ballet dancing. And you can forget about the f***ing boxing as well. I've been busting my arse for those fifty pences. You know how tight money is. You can stay here and look after your nan. Got it? Good.'

'I could have been a professional dancer if I'd had the chance,' said Nan.

'Will you shut up!' Dad turned round and roared at her, the sod. He had no business speaking to her like that.

I jumped right up and screamed in his face, 'I hate you! You're a bastard!' He made a lunge for me but I was away.

He was up and after me. 'Billy!' – but I was gone. Suddenly I had tears streaming down my face and I knew he'd just think I was being a poof all over again. I could hear him bellowing, but I'd had it with him, the bastard. I was out the door and up the street and across the field and down the beck and gone. Bastard! It was the only thing I'd ever been really good at and he was stopping me doing it. Bastard! Bastard, bastard! I ran for miles. That was it, that was really it. He meant it. If Dad says something like that, he sticks to it. If he caught me anywhere near the Social, he'd leather me. I ended up down on the beach, miles away. It was a big windy day, waves coming in crashing on the beach. I can understand why me nan comes down here. Just listening to the water munching away on the stones – it clears your head, calms you down. Helps you think. I started chucking stones at the waves and watching the water swallowing them up. The sun was going down. I'd been out hours.

There was Everington behind me on the hill. I was on the posh side of town. Miss's side. I wondered, if I'd been posh like her, I'd've been allowed to do ballet. But it wasn't that. I was the only boy in the class. Middle class, working class, it makes no difference. Boys don't do ballet, full stop.

There wasn't anything she could do about it.

Actually, her house was a lot smaller than I thought it'd be. I'd only ever seen those houses from the beach before. It was more of a bungalow than a house when you got up close. It had a garden at the front and a garage and all that, and it was on its own, not a terrace like ours, but when you got inside it was a lot smaller than you might think. I don't know why they bother building houses on their own unless they're bigger. I mean, what for?

I went up and knocked. I didn't know why. Me dad was me dad. What could she do? Middle-class Millie.

The door opened and there she was, breathing fag smoke.

'Oh. It's you, is it?' she said.

I said, 'He'd kill me if he knew I'd come here.'

'He's stopped you coming to classes, has he?'

'It's not his fault, miss,' I said.

'And that's fine by you, is it?'

I shrugged. 'I suppose so,' I said. I wasn't going to slag Dad off to her, I don't care what she thought of him. He's still me dad.

'You should stand up to him,' she said.

'You don't know what he's like, miss.'

'Well, that blows it,' she said, and she dragged on her fag and blew smoke all over me.

'Blimey, miss!' I said, trying to waft it away.

'Sorry.'

'Blows what?' I said, but she'd already turned back into the house.

'Debbie!' she yelled. 'It's Billy. Come and see to him, will you?'

I followed her into the sitting room. I don't think I'd been in a middle-class house before. It was funny. It was, like I say, not much bigger than ours and the furniture wasn't any better either. I don't know what I'd been expecting, antiques or something. But it was just normal stuff. Quite old. Tatty, really. I thought. Maybe it's not so bloody marvellous being middle class after all.

I sat down on the settee and in a bit Debbie came down and sat next to me. Her dad was sitting there hunched up in a chair with a drink in his mitt.

'Well, well, well,' he went. 'Everington's little Gene Kelly, isn't it? I've heard a lot about you. Your dad down the pit, is he?'

'Yeah.'

58

'Must be hard on the family being out on strike. He is out on strike, is he?'

'Course,' I said.

'Don't worry, son.' He stuck his nose in his drink and swallowed a mouthful. 'It won't take long.'

'Long as it takes,' I told him, and he glared at me.

'Tom, be quiet,' said Miss.

'If they had a ballot they'd be back tomorrow. It's just a few bloody commies stirring things up. Let's face it, they don't have a bloody leg to stand on. It stands to reason. Some pits just aren't economical. If it costs more money to pay blokes like your dad to dig the stuff up out of the ground than you get when you sell it, well. What does that tell you?'

I shrugged. I don't know what he was so cross about. You'd've thought my dad was out on strike just to get him. What difference did it make to him anyhow? I suppose he thought that just because I liked ballet, that made me think like him. Well, it didn't, did it?

Miss came out of the kitchen and started setting the table. 'Tom, don't go on at him.'

'Well, you wanna think about it, son. What sort of country is this going to be if people keep jobs that don't make any money, eh?'

'Tom!'

'If it were up to me, I'd close the lot of them down tomorrow.'

'Yeah, but it isn't up to you,' I said.

'Now listen, son –' he began, but Miss jumped in right off.

'I said leave him be, Tom,' she snapped. 'He's a guest here, not one of your friends down the pub.'

'What do you do, Mr Wilkinson?' I asked him.

'He's been made redundant,' said Debbie, before he could get a word in.

'Didn't you go out on strike to save your job, then?' I said and I swear, he blushed red like a little kid. I thought he was gonna jump up and lump me one. But he sat there scowling and frowning and he never said another word.

I had dinner there. Later on, up in her room, Debbie told me all about her mam and dad. We were sitting next to each other on her bed, and she had this little doll sat on her lap she was playing with, and she told me everything. It was none of my business really. She said her dad drank too much. She said once, he drank so much he pissed himself in the armchair and they had to get a new cushion for it. She said he'd had an affair, and he was unhappy because Miss wouldn't sleep with him.

'They have separate beds and everything,' she said.

'Does she not like sex, like?' I asked her.

'I think she used to like it,' Debbie said. 'Don't you miss your mam?'

Well, but I didn't want to tell her about my mam. I don't think about her most of the time. Sometimes I forget that she's dead. I go into the kitchen or one of the other rooms and I think she's just gone out to the shops, or that she's next door with my nan, or even once that she was bending down on the other side of the table picking something off the floor that had fallen down. But then she never stands up, and she never comes back from the shops, and when I go next door, my nan's in there on her own. It seems impossible that my mam's not there any more. Maybe that's what she means in her letter, when she says she's there for me for ever, even though she's dead. Maybe she really is there all the time but I just can't see her.

But I never said any of that to Debbie. 'So does your mam not have sex at all, then?' I asked her.

'No. She's unfulfilled. That's why she does dancing.'

I couldn't believe my ears. I said, 'You mean she does dancing instead of sex? Your family's weird!' I always thought that if you were middle class and you had a mam and a dad and all, then that was all normal, like. But instead of that, here I was in a middle-class house and it was all completely weird.

'No, they're not,' said Debbie. She put her doll down and shifted over closer to me. She was so close we were almost touching and it made me feel uncomfortable. I moved away slightly.

'They are, though,' I said. 'They're all mental.'

She shuffled up closer again, so I bonked her on the head with a pillow. She ducked round to grab one and we had this great pillow fight, whacking each other with the pillows. I didn't do it too hard, though. She was just a girl, I didn't want to hurt her. I kept pushing her away and holding her wrists with one hand and bopping her with the other, and then I climbed on top of her and sat on her legs. She was screeching and giggling. And then, you know, while I was struggling for her hands, my hand brushed against her top and I felt her tits. I never realised she had tits yet, they were only small. It was a bit of a shock. I stopped and she stopped and we looked at each other. It felt funny, then, sitting on top of her. She reached up and stroked my face. It felt nice, she was very gentle but it was embarrassing because – you know – it made my willy go stiff.

I got off.

'See. You're a nutter, you,' I told her.

She sat up and looked the other way. I didn't know what to do. There was feathers floating on the air where the pillow had leaked. I wafted them at her so they landed on her jumper, and she sat there picking them off.

'Debbie, it's time for Billy to go home.' It was Miss calling up the stairs. I jumped up. What would she say if she thought I'd been touching her daughter's tits in her bedroom? Even though I never meant it.

'Come on, Billy, I'll give you a lift to the corner.'

'See you, Debbie.'

'Bye, Billy.'

She sat there with her hands on her lap not looking at me as I walked out the door.

Miss gave me a lift just round the corner from where I lived. She would've taken me all the way home but I didn't want to get caught in her car. She pulled up on some waste ground near our house.

'Right then,' she said. I didn't move, though. I just sat there for a bit. We hadn't said anything about it, not really. She turned the car off, sighed, and took herself a fag out.

'This'll sound strange. Billy,' she said. 'But I was thinking of auditioning for the Royal Ballet School.'

I thought, Jesus, she's keen on that dancing then. I thought – I know this is stupid but it was just after that talk with Debbie, like – I thought it must be having no sex was making her want to do something stupid like that.

'Aren't you a bit old, miss?' I asked her.

She snorted. 'Not me, Billy. You. I'm the teacher. Christ!' She rolled her eyes. 'They hold auditions in Newcastle,' she said, and gave me a long look.

Ballet school? Me? But that'd be . . . something else. I mean, it was a hobby, that's all. But if you went to a special school . . .

'Can you do it as a job, then, miss?'

'Course you can. If you're good enough.'

'I'd never be good enough. I hardly know owt.'

'Look.' She twisted round in her seat to face me and blew a spurt of smoke over her shoulder. 'Listen. They're not interested in how much ballet you know. They teach you that. That's why they're a ballet school. It's how you move, how you express yourself that's important.'

'Express what?' I didn't know what she meant. It's just dancing, isn't it?

'I think you're good enough,' she said. And that was the only time she ever told me I was any good. 'It'd be an awful lot of work,' she said.

'I'm banned,' I reminded her.

'Aye, well. Maybe I should have a word with him.'

'No!' I almost jumped out of the seat. 'Miss! Don't.'

'For god's sake.' She puffed away on her fag for a bit, then she said, 'You know, I could teach you on your own if you want.'

'I've got no money.'

'I'm not doing it for the money,' she snapped, as if I'd offended her.

'But what about Dad?'

'He doesn't have to know, does he?'

'What about me boxing and that?' I wasn't asking her just about the boxing, like. I wasn't even allowed to do that any more. It was about . . . being one of the lads. You know. Being a boy. That sort of thing.

'For f***'s sake, Billy. If you want to piss around

64

with your little mates, that's fine by me. This is serious.'

'All right, don't lose your blob.'

'Blob?' she said, and we both laughed.

I thought about it a bit. It was a bit much, wasn't it? Doing things behind me dad's back and that. Training to be a ballet dancer. But – wow! You know? That'd be summat, wouldn't it?

'So we could do it in private, like?'

'Just you and me. No one else need know.'

I dunno. Behind me dad's back. And her doing dancing instead of sex, it was all a bit . . .

'Miss, you don't fancy me or owt, do you?'

She turned and stared at me in amazement. Then she looked furious. 'No, Billy, I do not fancy you, strange to say. Now piss off, will you?'

I stared at her. She was really cross. There was a long pause. She nodded at the door. 'Go on, then,' she told me.

I thought, f★★★ it. What had I got to lose?

'Piss off yourself,' I said. Then I smiled at her, and she smiled back. I turned to get out of the car

'See you Monday, then,' she said. 'Six o'clock at the Social Hall. I'll be waiting.'

I didn't say yea or nay. I just stood there facing away from her with the door still open.

'And bring something with you. Something personal. Anything you want. Something to give us an idea for the dance.'

'What dance?'

'Your audition dance, blockhead.'

I shut the door and she drove off. I thought. What am I getting into? I still hadn't got a clue if I was going to go there or not.

MICHAEL

The doorbell went and I sneaked to the bedroom window for a peek down. I was wearing a violet frock, a pair of tights, me mam's red shoes and a little crocheted cardigan me sister used to wear. It looked outrageous. If it'd been anyone else down there I'd've pretended I was out.

I thought, I'll show him. I'll show Billy Elliot. Well, he couldn't say owt, could he? He's the bloody ballet dancer, not me.

I ran downstairs and opened the door and he nearly fell backwards off the step. Then he pushed me back in through the door before anyone saw.

'What are you doing, man?'

'Nothing, just dressing up,' I said.

'Whose dress is that?'

'Me sister's. Are you coming up or what?'

He followed me up the stairs to Mam's bedroom. 'Eh, you,' I told him. 'Are you trying to look up my dress, you dirty little bugger?'

'Get off. Has she given it to you?'

'She doesn't know. All right, man, it's just a bit of fun. Look!' I did a little swirl and curtsied.

He was worrying me, he looked so scared. You know what I felt like doing? Just to scare him, like? I felt like running across and giving him a big kiss. That'd scare him half to death. Billy Elliot! What's he got to talk about?

'If you can prance about in ballet gear, I can wear me sister's clothes, can't I?'

'I don't prance about in ballet gear.'

'What do you wear, then? Don't you wear one of them tutus?'

'No, you dope, they're just for the girls.'

'What do you wear then?' I asked him.

'Just me sports gear. My shorts and T-shirt and that.'

'Really?' I'd thought he must wear a tutu or something like it. But it was just his shorts and his T-shirt. I think, you know, if I'd known that I might not have let him see me wearing me sister's gear. But it was too late now. I began to root about in the wardrobe for something that'd suit Billy. It'd be a right gas if I got him to dress up too.

'What about this one?' I pulled out a skirt, but he shook his head. 'No? I suppose it's not really your colour, is it?'

'I don't care whose colour it is, I'm not wearing a bloody skirt.'

'I thought you'd like it.'

'Just because I dance doesn't mean to say I'm a poof, you poof.'

'Just because I'm wearing me sister's dress doesn't make me one, either, you poof.'

I said that just to stick up for meself, but to tell you truth I do wonder about myself sometimes. I mean, putting on my sister's stuff, that's just a gas. It doesn't turn me on or owt. On the other hand . . . well. I like Billy. I like it when he shows me his dance moves under the old bridge when we should be doing cross-country. I like it when he jumps and spins. I like it when he sits close and tells me his secrets and when we have little fights. So I do wonder about meself. But he doesn't have to know that, does he?

I put the skirt back and went over to me mam's dressing table where the make-up was, and I dusted a bit of blusher onto me cheeks. I was doing it to tease him as much as anything.

'What are you doing now?' said Billy.

'I'm just trying it on.'

'Christ.'

I smiled at him in the mirror and he smiled back. It was just a gas. I was a bit disappointed he didn't want to join in, though.

'Come here, you.' I jumped up and grabbed him, shoved him back onto the bed.

'Gerroff!'

'Stay still!'

He did as I said, and I started to put lipstick on him. It was funny – him sitting there holding his face up to me while I put it on. You know what? He looked good. It really changes your face, lipstick. I wonder that more men don't do it. It's quite fashionable nowadays to wear make-up. He had nice lips,

Billy – a pretty bow on top. The colour suited him and all.

'Won't we get into trouble?' he asked. He got up and looked in the mirror.

'Nah.'

'Eh, Michael, look!' He leaned forward and kissed the mirror. There was a lovely kiss shape on the glass. Billy leaned forward to have a better look.

'Just like a girl's kiss,' he said.

'Girls' lips and boys' lips are just the same,' I told him.

'Do you reckon?'

I stared at the kiss. I wanted to kiss the kiss, but I didn't. 'It's just the lipstick and stuff makes them look different.'

'You're weird. What if we get caught?'

'Don't be daft. My dad does it all the time.'

It's true. Well, not all the time, but I have seen him wearing make-up and putting me mam's clothes on and stuff. There was no one else in the house, he thought I was out. He was just doing it to please himself, I reckon. If he did it once, I reckon he must do it all the time.

'Really?' Billy was amazed.

'All the time,' I told him. I just wanted him to know it was perfectly normal. I'll bet everyone does it when they think no one's looking. It's fun.

Billy sat down at the dressing table and looked at himself in the mirror.

'Michael, do you think being a ballet dancer would be better than being a miner?' he said.

That was a tough one. 'I dunno,' I told him.

'It's just . . . I've got this audition in Newcastle in a couple of weeks.'

'What for?'

'For to go to ballet school.'

'Ballet school? In Newcastle?'

'London.'

'Would you have to go with your Tony and everybody?'

'No, I'd have to go on me own.'

'Eh, that's a bit steep. Can't you be a ballet dancer here, then?'

'Divvint be stupid.'

Aye. Ballet in Newcastle! No chance of that. You know, when he first started dancing he asked me to join in with him, but I said, No way! No way! Can you imagine it? You have to admire him, though. He's always getting teased at school and that. Kids picking on him. But he was never scared of a fight, our Billy. Well, he'd never have stuck with the ballet if he was, would he, because he was bound to get one. Round here it's about the quickest way of getting your face kicked in, I reckon.

Look at me. I'd run a mile to get out of a fight, it's a waste of time. But people are always picking on me anyhow. If there was something I could give up that would stop people picking on me, I'd do it. But there's not. You can't give up being just

71

yourself. My dad always says that I'm different and I should be proud of it, but round here being different isn't such a good thing at all. It's a bloody problem. In infants I was always getting picked on. In primary I was always getting picked on. We're going to be starting high school soon and I'm going to be picked on there and all, I bet you.

But Billy's always been a good friend to me. He never minded me being different. I don't know why, I always thought he wasn't at all different himself, he always seemed to be exactly the same as everyone else except that he stood up for me instead of picking on me. I always thought he could have got on with any of them, except for some reason he'd ended up with me, like a sort of accident. Like he'd made friends with me before he realised how weird I was and then just stuck with me. It always used to worry me that one day he'd realise I was all wrong and drop me, but he never did. And then he took up ballet and after that he was just as weird as I was, and I stopped worrying about it.

And now here he was planning on going down to London to be a ballet dancer.

'So when are you going?' I asked him.

'I don't know, I haven't even got in yet. It might never happen.'

I thought about it. 'So what does your dad say, then?'

'Doesn't know.'

'Are you not going to tell him?'

'Not yet, anyhow. He'll go f***ing mental.'

'No, he won't, he'll be pleased, then he can rent your room out,' I told him. I was just joking, but Billy looked really pissed off.

'Don't say that,' he told me. 'Anyhow,' he added, 'he couldn't rent it out – what about our Tony? It's his room and all.'

I wandered back off to the wardrobe and rooted about for more frocks. I didn't really want another frock, I was hiding me face. I was upset. I wanted to say, 'Don't go, Billy, I'll be left all on me own.'

'What do you reckon?' he asked me.

'I think you shouldn't bother,' I told him.

'Why not?'

I glanced round at him. 'Well, I'd miss you,' I said.

'Oh, bloody hell, Michael!'

'Well, it's true,' I told him. I wasn't being much use, really. I suppose he just wanted some advice. I was being selfish, but what do I know about London and ballet school and that? I don't know anything. But I knew I'd miss him if he went away. I was feeling lonely already.

Billy started cleaning his lipstick off. He wanted me to come out and muck around but I didn't feel like it. I was thinking, shit, shit, shit. If Billy goes away, who can I talk to then? And who'll want to talk to me?

As usual, I think he felt sorry for me, because he said, 'Tell you what, I'll show you.' He pushed back the chair and made a little space next to the bed and started going through the moves. 'Come on,' he said, 'and you. Bend your legs. Plie. Like this.'

'What's that?'

'It's French.'

'Why's it French?'

'I don't f***ing know! Look, like this. Beautiful neck. Like a princess, you poof.'

He showed me the moves and I followed what he was doing. I'm not that type myself, but I enjoyed watching him go through it. He half closed his eyes and he seemed to forget that I was wearing a dress and pretending to be a girl. He just went through the moves one after the other, murmuring, 'Up and round and one and two . . .' to himself. He looked really lovely, lost in his own little world. Then he jumped up and did this spin like a f***ing top. It almost made me shout.

'F*** ya!' he yelled, and he went round and round so fast he nearly took my head off.

'Wow,' I said, and he grinned at me.

'How about that, then?' he said. 'How about that? That's dancing, ain't it?'

BILLY

Everything happened all at once. We only had two weeks before the audition. We went at it like maniacs.

There were those things she asked me to bring in – something personal, she said. I'd never made up a dance before, I'd no idea – how do you start something like that? I just grabbed what was there, like. A Newcastle United shirt, a football – I thought maybe I could do something with that – you know, boot it around or something. Why shouldn't that be part of the dance? There was a tape: 'I Like to Boogie' by T. Rex. It's one of our Tony's. I was hoping she could copy it for me, he'd kill me if he found out. It just seemed like something I'd like to dance to.

And me mam's letter.

I don't know why I brought along mam's letter. Well, I do – it's because she said bring something personal and there's nothing more personal to me than that. But I felt funny about it. I mean, it's none of her business, is it? It's none of anyone's business except mine.

I met her round at the Social by the boxing ring

that Monday, like we'd arranged, and she started to go through the things. I was a bit worried they might be wrong, but she said so long as they were special to me, it was all right. She didn't think much of the football idea. She just gave a sniff and said, 'Do you fancy chasing this around? What if it goes the wrong way? You'll feel a right prat then, won't you? How good are your ball skills?'

'Not bad,' I said, but she chucked the ball to one side anyhow. Then she picked up the letter and looked at me oddly. Of course, it was the letter she was going to go for. I knew she bloody would. I was afraid of it.

'It was supposed to be for when I was eighteen,' I told her, 'but I opened it early.'

She took it out and began to read. 'Dear Billy.' Then she stopped and looked at me again. 'Do you mind if I read it out?'

'I suppose not,' I said.

'I know I must seem like a distant memory to you. Which is probably a good thing,' she read. 'It will have been a long time. And I will have missed seeing you grow, missed you crying and laughing and shouting . . .'

She sort of stared at me and stopped, so I carried on for her.

'I will have missed telling you off,' I said. 'But please know that I was always there, with you all through everything. And I always will be. And I am proud to have known you. And I am proud that you were mine. Always be yourself. I love you for ever.'

I didn't need to read it, I knew it by heart. Miss looked at the end of it to see if that was it and then read the last word.

'Mam.'

She looked the other way and started breathing heavily. 'Are you all right, Miss?' I asked. Then she sniffed and rubbed her nose on her arm and I knew, she was crying. I thought, Oh, Jesus, I shouldn't have brought it in. The whole thing's going to be totally soppy now I've done that.

'She must have been a very, very special woman, Billy,' she said at last.

'Nah, she was just me mam,' I said.

She started asking me questions about her then – what sort of things she liked, what made her happy, what made her sad. I kept trying to tell her about the tape. It's the music I was interested in. In the end I got round her by saying, 'Mam liked music too. She was a piano player. She liked rock 'n' roll. She was always asking our Tony to put this on.' So she put the tape on then and we sat together on the edge of the boxing ring and listened to it.

'I like to boogie,' sang Marc Bolan.

'Jitterbug boogie.

'I like to boogie

'On a Saturday night.'

'Happy music,' she said. 'Foot-tapping music.'

'Dancing music,' I told her.

'Your mam liked this, you say?'

'Aye.'

'She liked being happy. Was she kind?'

'Of course she was. She used to get a bit stressed, that's all.'

'Don't we all. So. Happy, kind, stressed. And foot-tapping. That's our dance, Billy. Right, let's get going. Put that tape on again.'

We had fun that day! We jiggled and jumped and ran round in circles. She made me arse about. She never let me arse about before, it was always, you had to do things exactly like she said, exactly right. Now suddenly we were mucking around around. I had to show her how mam did this daft dance she used to do for a laugh. I had to show what she was like when she did ballet with me nan. I had to show her what she was like when she was being cross, and how she tipped her head back when she laughed. It was dead clever, actually. She got all those movements and then sort of strung them together. There was even a bit of footy in it too, and a whole lot of foot-tapping – and that was our dance!

'Now listen, Billy,' she told me. 'When you're dead, you're dead, and that's it. But I want to imagine, just imagine, mind, that you're dancing your mam right back to life. And at the end of it you're going to do the biggest, fastest, highest spin any living child ever did do, and when you do that spin, you'll be whizzing round so fast you'll be able to catch your mam out the corner of your eye clapping her hands and jumping up out of her chair in excitement, just like you showed me just now. Right?'

'Right!' I said. Actually, I thought that was a bit much. Telling me to dance Mam back to life. I can just imagine what Tony would say if he knew that, he'd want to smack her one. But the thing about Miss is, she's clever. It worked, see. I thought about Mam and dancing so hard she'd jump up and clap – and it worked. Even though I thought she was being a bit cheeky, really.

I knew she'd latch onto Mam, but the great thing about it was, it wasn't soppy. One thing you had to say about Miss, she was really not soppy. It was a right happy dance. It made you feel good. It made you feel – foot-tapping!

'I love to boogie,
Jitterbug boogie.
I love to boogie
On a Saturday night, night. All right!'

At home, things were going right the other way.

It wasn't just home, mind. The whole bloody town was under siege. You'd have thought we were trying to attack the Houses of Parliament rather than just be out on strike. The police were everywhere.

When it started off they were just down by the pit. They were OK at first, they used to chat with the miners, everything was fairly friendly. But then miners from other places were coming to picket our pit, and that's when they started. There were

79

road blocks and all sorts. They were everywhere. Gangs of them wandering around all over the place. On horseback. In cars. On motorbikes. All over our town.

It wasn't getting them anywhere, though, we were running rings around them. The miners always found a way to get to the pit no matter how hard the police tried to stop them. They hid on the school buses and lorries taking goods to the shops. We had people from all over, not just miners, coming in to fight for the mines. Young people, old people, all sorts, all gathered round the pit chanting, 'Here we go, here we go, here we go' and 'Maggie Maggie Maggie – out out out!' Tony reckoned we were going to bring the government down, but we had no money left at all. People were chopping down anything you could burn just to keep warm. We pulled our little wooden shed in the yard to bits for firewood. We were – well, I never went hungry but I was geting really sick of sliced bread and marge. I'd have died for a bacon buttie. There was nothing to spare, no treats, no money for anything. They were trying to starve us out, see. And frighten us and all, with the police. It was scary.

It was the ones on horseback that scared me the most. They were so big, and the policemen had these long sticks to hit people with. You know? Galloping up behind one of the miners and whack! Right across their backs or round the head. There was blood and everything. I've seen it. You'd never ask a policeman the time again if you'd seen them do what I have.

What's got four legs and an arsehole in the middle of its back? A police horse.

Our Tony told me that one. I was getting on better with him lately, maybe it was because we were both not getting on with Dad. I was pissed off with him because he wasn't letting me dance. Tony was pissed off with him because he was a silly old bastard who'd had all the juice sucked out of him. That's what he said. He was always shouting at him. Dad never said much back, he just let him go on. I felt sorry for him, it wasn't his fault the mines were being closed down. But Tony was right. He's just a silly old bloke. Stuck in a time warp.

He stuck up for himself when Tony pushed him too far, though.

It was the middle of the night, just about a week away from the audition. I was woken up by Tony getting out of bed.

'What're you doing? What's the time?' I asked.

'Shurrup, get back to sleep,' he told me. He was standing there pulling his jeans on, trying to be dead quiet. I looked at the clock. It was four in the morning. What was he up to, this time of night?

'Get back to bed!' he hissed. I lay back down and rolled over. He tiptoed out. I lay back down and listened. A couple of minutes later the shouting started and I got up to have a look.

Dad was standing in front of the back door. Tony was in front of him, white as a sheet. He had a bloody great hammer in his hand.

'Get out of my way,' Tony was saying. He was bloody furious.

'Put that down.'

'I said, get out of my way!'

'Put it away.'

Tony suddenly lost it. He rushed up to Dad waving the hammer right under his nose. I thought he was going to lump him with it.

'No!' I shouted, but they both hardly glanced at me.

'You wanna just stand around getting the shit kicked out of you, that's your problem,' Tony yelled. He was pushing his face right up to Dad's. 'Fine. But some of us are ready to fight back for once. You might be finished but I've only just f***ing begun. Now – get out of my way!'

Dad just stood there like a rock. 'You're no use to us in jail,' he said.

'I'm not planning on getting caught.'

'What are you doing?' I cried.

'Get back to bed – both of you!' roared Dad. Tony took a step back. He was almost ready to do as he was told, like he was a kid again. But then he lifted up the hammer and stopped himself.

'F*** you,' he said.

'Put it down!'

'Are you going to make me?'

'I'm warning you.'

'You haven't f***ing got it in you! You're finished, aren't you? Since Mam died you're nothing but a useless old idiot. Stop me then! What are you gonna do about it, eh?'

He made to push Dad to one side, but Dad had had enough. He suddenly pulled his arm back – it was so quick I hardly saw it – and then, bang! He got Tony right on the side of his face. Tony went down like a log.

'Stop it! Stop it!' I screamed.

Dad turned to look at me. I'd never seen him look like that. He was white and red and his eyes were shining like he'd gone mad. 'What the f*** are you looking at?' he yelled. I backed off – I was scared he was going to turn on me. I never saw him so angry. Tony picked himself off the floor and staggered forward at Dad. For a moment I thought he was going to use the hammer on him, but he just shouldered him to one side and ran out the door.

'You're not concentrating, Billy! Billy! Chin up!'
'What?'

That was Miss. I was lifting up my arms and holding my chin up but all I could see was Tony and Dad – that hammer in Dad's face. Dad's face so white and red. Dad's fist going smack into Tony, Tony falling.

It was all I could think of all day long.
'Billy!'
. . . Dad's fist going back and bang! . . .

'You're not concentrating!'

'I am, miss, I am concentrating.'

'You're not even trying!'

It was stuck in my mind. That hammer in Dad's face . . .

'Do it again!'

'What?' Dad's fist – bang!

'Do it again!'

'I can't!'

'You do it again! You do it again right now!'

She had her face right up into mine. She was as bloody bad as they were, practically spitting on me, that dirty fag smoking away in my eyes.

'I said, you do it again.'

. . . 'No.'

'What?' She took a step back, like she couldn't believe what she'd just heard.

'No,' I said again, and then that was it. I'd had enough. On and on and on and on and on at me, the bloody old bitch. I ran out of there and into the changing rooms. Didn't I have enough on my plate? She thought my whole life was built around her – well, it wasn't! I ran into a cubicle and locked the door. Sometimes you just . . . well. I couldn't get it out of my mind, could I? That hammer. He was bloody going to smash my dad with it. With a f***ing hammer! What was going on? And Dad, smacking him like that. Fighting each other, pulling everything to pieces. If our mam was here, it'd be different. She'd never let Tony and Dad go on at each other like that.

Everything had fallen to pieces ever since she died.

The door to the changing rooms opened. That old door is as squeaky as anything. She came walking down past the cubicles. She couldn't see which one I was in. There was a gap under the doors but I had me feet up on the bench so she couldn't see me.

'Billy?'

I was saying nowt.

'I know you're in there Billy. Billy, I'm sorry.'

Sorry, she says. What good's that? I'd really had it with her. I banged the door open and jumped out on her, sudden like. I made her jump and all.

'It's all right for you, it's not you who has to do it!'

She looked scared. I was almost as big as she was. Actually, I was bigger.

'I know,' she said. 'I get carried away.'

'You don't know bloody anything,' I shouted. 'Sitting there in your posh house with your husband that pisses hisself. You're the same as everyone else, all you want is to tell me what to do.'

'Now wait a minute, who do you think I'm doing this for?'

'Well, I don't want to go to your stupid f***ing audition. You only want me to do it for your own bloody benefit . . .'

'Now, look here, Billy,' she said, but I wasn't having any of it.

'Just because you're a failure!'

'Don't you dare talk to me like that!'

'You don't even have a proper dancing school. You're just stuck in some crummy school gym and you just pick on me because you f★★★ed up your own life –'

That's when she slapped me. Whack, right round the chops. Really hard. It bloody hurt. I was shocked. I never thought she'd do that. She had no business doing that. I put my hand to me face. She looked as shocked as I was. I took a step back; she took a step forward and held her arms out.

'Billy, love,' she said. Well, I was ready to run. I was ready to go out that door and never come back. But . . .

Well, it wasn't her fault, was it? If I didn't keep her, what had I got? I didn't want to stop dancing, you see. So I couldn't leave. And because I couldn't leave, I started crying instead. She took another step towards me and reached out for my head when she saw my eyes go wet, and I let her put my head on her shoulder. I leaned against her like a pudding and just cried.

'I'm sorry, Billy,' she said. 'I'm really sorry.' And me, I just cried my head off while she stroked my haircut. It went on for about five minutes.

'Right,' she said at last. 'Have you done?'

'Yes, miss. Sorry,' I said. She pushed my head back up and I wiped my eyes on my T-shirt.

'Good lad,' she said. She pulled out a fag from

the packet in her pocket and lit it in the corner of her mouth. 'Let's get back to it, shall we?'

You've got to hand it to her, haven't you? And you know what? She never even asked me what the matter was.

Well, but I was glad she did make me, because the dance was the one thing that was going right for me. I wasn't doing well at school, either. I mean, not bad, but not all that good, you know? But the dance was going well and I felt good about that.

On the other hand, the audition was getting closer and I felt really bad about that. It was scary, you know? Trying for something like that. If it worked, if I passed, what then? I'd have to tell me dad and he'd go mental. And even if he let me, then what? Leave home? Go to live all the way in London on me own? No way! It was bonkers. What was it going to cost? Christ!

But I had me dad right fooled. I was doing ballet every night and he never had a clue. He thought I was out playing with Michael. I had it all arranged. Michael'd come and call for me, or I'd go round to his, and we'd go out together as if we were just hanging around together. He'd even come into the Social with me, but then he'd sneak out the back way and go off to do whatever it was he did with himself on his own – dressing up or whatever, I expect, the big pansy.

You know, I wonder about Michael. I wonder if

maybe he really is a poof and maybe he thinks I might be one too, because I like ballet. Well, I'm not, no way, but something happened a little while ago that worried me, with that Debbie. She used to come along sometimes to watch me do my stuff. She was jealous because Miss was her mam but she wasn't putting Debbie in for the Royal Ballet School. When I asked her why not, Miss just shrugged and said she wasn't good enough. Anyhow, this one day, I was pulling my top on after the dance, I was all sweaty and stinky, but I was happy, because it'd gone really well that day. Debbie was sitting there sucking a lollipop and watching me.

'Billy,' she said. 'Do you not fancy me at all?'

'I dunno,' I said. I mean, I'd never really thought about it. It made my heart start beating, though, because I was scared she was going to ask me to go out with her. One thing I was clear about, I didn't want to go out with Debbie Wilkinson. Debbie's pretty bloody odd herself, if you ask me. If I had to have a girlfriend, it wouldn't be her, that's all.

By the week of the audition, I was more scared than I'd ever been in my whole life. I still hadn't told me dad. The audition was on the Saturday morning at half ten. He didn't have to know, I didn't need time off school or owt. I just thought, Well, if I don't get in, he never has to know, and if I do – well, maybe he'll bloody kill me, but maybe he'll be so amazed that I've actually gone and done it that he'll let me go.

Anyway, I couldn't believe I was ever going to get it. I kept saying to Miss, 'It's a waste of time, miss, I won't get in.'

'Yes, you bloody will, Billy Elliot, you'll get in if it's the last thing I do. You'll sail in. They'll never have seen anything like you, and that's the truth. Right! Let's get on.'

There was no one to talk to about it. She was no use, all she ever did was push. There was Michael, he was OK, but . . . well, it made me miss Mam, that's all. I could have talked to her about it. She'd have known what to say, what to do. She was the only person in the world I could have talked to, and she wasn't bloody there. See, all that stuff in her letter was just tripe, really. She was dead. Dead and stopped. She couldn't tell me anything, could she? She couldn't even hear anything. I don't blame her for writing that letter. I suppose it was to make her feel better, and to make me feel better too, but it was tripe all the same.

And then this thing happened. It was just a couple of days before the audition. You won't believe me. I don't believe it all that much myself, but it did happen and there you go, and I'm going to tell you anyhow.

The audition was half past ten on Saturday morning, and this was the Thursday before. The Social was being used for a fundraising event for the miners that evening, so we drove out to this school where she knew someone and used their gym and we had to go across on the transporter bridge. It's an old iron thing made of girders, and instead of spanning the river it has this carriage which gets hauled across, first one way, then the other.

On the way back, we were waiting in the car for the transporter to come and I was bored, so I asked if I could put a tape on. Miss was fagging away as usual. She smoked as if the whole world was waiting for her to finish her fag and she had to really concentrate on it to get it done properly.

'If you must,' she said.

There was one lying on the dashboard. It didn't have any name on it, it was one she must've made. I put it on. It was classical stuff – not something I'd ever usually listen to. Rock and pop was more my kind of thing, but – maybe it was because I'd been hearing that sort of thing on the piano from Mr Braithwaite during class, I dunno, but I listened to it this time. And you know what? I liked it. Once you got into it, it was really something else.

She sat there watching me listen for a bit. Then she stubbed her fag out and turned the sound up. The transporter came over and we drove on, then we sat still and listened.

The thing was, I knew that music. I'd heard it before, I'm sure I had. Maybe I'd heard it on the radio years and years ago when I was still a little kid, and I'd never paid any attention to it. Not like now. Now the music came out and filled up the car, and it filled me up too. It was beautiful. It was fantastic.

Then the tape ran out.

'Sorry,' she said. 'It's off the radio. I didn't get all of it.'

'It's cush, innit?' I said. 'What is it? Is there a story?'

'Swan Lake,' she said. 'It's a ballet. Of course there's a story. It's about this woman who gets captured by this evil magician.'

I pulled a face. I might have known. 'Sounds crap,' I said. But Miss was on a roll. It really meant something to her.

'This woman, this beautiful woman, she's turned into a swan, you see, except for a few hours every night when she becomes alive. I mean, when she becomes herself again. When she becomes real. And then one night she meets this young prince and he falls in love with her, and she realises that this is the one thing that'll allow her to become a person again. A real woman.'

I looked sideways at her. She was really looking flushed. I don't know why some old story should make her feel like that.

'So what happens?' I said.

'He promises to marry her and then goes with someone else, of course. The usual.' I had to smile to myself, because she looked all sour again – back to her usual self.

'So she has to be a swan for good, then?'

'She dies.'

'That's a bit steep. Because the prince didn't really love her?'

'Come on, it's time to go. It's only a ghost story.' And she started up the car and drove off.

It was dark by the time I got home. It was getting cold – the leaves were all off the trees, it was just about winter. The house was freezing cold because we couldn't afford to turn the central heating on. We'd finished burning up the old shed ages ago. I put me dressing gown on over me clothes to keep warm. Dad and Terry were out, which was odd; I remember wondering, where on earth were they? Dad was always in at that time. The do at the Social should have finished. Nan was in, that was all. I went to peep in through the sliding door to her room to see if she was all right.

'No!' she shouted when she heard the door open. 'No. No.' It was one of her bad days.

'It's only me, Nan,' I said. I waited for her to recognise me, but she just stared. 'It's Billy,' I said. She lay back down.

I went back to the kitchen and opened the fridge. I don't know why we bother keeping the fridge on, it costs money and the place is so cold it's like a fridge anyway, you could keep the food on the table and it wouldn't be any colder.

I took out some milk and had a swig.

'Oi. Little 'un.'

I turned round. It was Mam. She was standing

there with a glass bowl in one hand and a cloth in the other, wiping the bowl clean. 'What have I told you about drinking out of the bottle?' she said.

'Sorry, Mam,' I said. I thought nothing of it. It was just like normal. I took a glass from the table and poured myself a glass properly, like, and put the bottle on top of the fridge while I drank it.

'Well, put it back,' she said.

I picked up the bottle, opened the door, put the milk back, turned around and she was gone and . . .

It was only then that I realised. It was only then. Mam. She'd been there. The bowl and the cloth were lying there on the table where she'd been. I walked over and picked up the bowl and it was still warm where her hands had been on it. See? It wasn't a ghost, she was real. I looked behind me. I wasn't scared. I knew she wasn't there any more so I didn't call for her or owt. I just stood there, not thinking. Then the sliding door opened and Nan came out.

'Now, Billy, it's in here,' she said. I thought, typical, I've just seen me mam and now Nan's having a barmy. She tottered over to the cupboard near where Mam had been standing and bent down to open the door.

'What, Nan?'

'The records, you dope.' She took a record out of the cupboard and grinned at me. She tapped her nose. 'I know,' she said. Then she turned and went next door.

'What do you know, Nan? What do you know?' I asked her. I followed her. She was in the front room putting a record on.

'Listen,' she said. The needle came down, the music came on.

Swan Lake. Same as I listened to an hour before with Miss.

I just stared at her. How had she known? You see – that's where I'd heard it before. It was one of Mam's old records. She had a box of records she used to play from time to time when I was small. No one ever played them now, they'd been put away to keep them safe for years.

'Did you see her too, Nan?' I asked. But Nan was gone. She began moving around the room, dancing. I'd seen her do those movements loads of times before, but I knew what they were now. Plie. Ballet. She used to do ballet when she was a girl.

'Like this,' I said. I came over to her and took her arms and we went through a few moves together, me and me nan. It was amazing. She was slow and stiff, but she knew what she was doing all right. Maybe she was right, maybe she did use to be good, once upon a time, long ago. We did a slow dance together, and it really was quite beautiful.

Then the door banged and before I could do owt, there was Tony standing in the door with me dad peering in over his shoulder.

'Who told you you could use my record player?' he said.

'It's not yours, it's Mam's,' I complained.

'You don't have any records, it's no use to you,' he said. He went over and took the needle off, all rough so it scratched.

'Oh, we were dancing to that,' complained Nan.

Then me dad joined in. 'You be bloody careful,' he yelled. I thought he was shouting at me, but it was Tony he was cross with for scratching Mam's record. 'You take a bit more care with things that aren't your own,' he told him. He took the record off him and wiped it carefully on his shirt-sleeve.

'No one ever plays it anyhow,' said Tony.

'And you,' said me dad to me. 'Who told you to play this?'

'Sorry,' I muttered.

'I could have been a professional dancer,' said Nan, and she did a little curtsey. Dad turned away and banged the door on his way out. It was horrible the way the two of them came banging in like that. I felt more sorry for Nan than anything, but it didn't matter to me, not just then, anyhow. I knew what it was about, see. Mam wanted me to go for it. That's what it meant. And I knew then, if Mam thought I should go for it, that maybe it wasn't just a stupid dream. Maybe it really could come true.

On the other hand, maybe I was just going bonkers meself, like Nan was. But now I was going to go for it as hard as I could. I was going to do me best.

The audition was the next morning at half past ten, and I felt ready to do anything for it – for me and for Mam. I went in on Friday afternoon after school to do the final practice, and it went perfect. I was up for anything. And then on the way home, there was a bloody riot.

TONY

It was my own fault in the first place for setting fire to that horse's arse.

I wasn't sorry for the horse. I know, it's a dumb animal, it can't help it if the coppers use it as an offensive weapon. But think about it – if it was about three hundred years ago and you was a peasant and you had one of those knights in shining armour bearing down on you on a bloody great charger, and it was question of him taking your head off or you swinging your spade into the horse's front legs, what would you do? No bloody contest, is it? It's the same thing. That horse was on their side, no matter what. It was the f***ing enemy.

Anyhow, it wasn't just any horse. That one wasn't so dumb, it was a bastard. It was always side-stepping into the crowd and getting on people's feet and kicking out at us. You ask anyone. It was going to have someone's head off. The horse and the piece of copper-shite on its back were well matched and all, they were bastards together. I wish it had been his arse I'd set fire to. I wish he'd farted himself to Kingdom bloody Come.

They don't have to be like that. Most of them are bastards – waving their big fat wage packets in our faces, all bloated up with the overtime they get paid for kicking our arses for Thatcher. But some of them are all right. I mean, they're all the bloody enemy as far as I'm concerned, as far as the working man's concerned, but some of them are half decent. Some of 'em didn't really want to be there, I reckon – not that it stopped them, mind.

'You're on the wrong bloody side,' I said to one of them.

'Yeah, well, I haven't got the option of striking, have I?'

'Well, you've sold out then, haven't you?' I said. And then we all started up, pointing at this kid and chanting, 'SOLD OUT! SOLD OUT! SOLD OUT!' Kid didn't know which way to look.

Alan Tattersley, him that used to have that little toy policeman's helmet he used to wear on the picket line, he just about almost converted one of them. He used to stick his great big hairy ugly face right up into the police line with that stupid little helmet on, like a great big kid, and every now and then one of them would crack up and start laughing. There was this one young lad started snorting and giggling to himself – he looked a right laugh, did Al, dressed up like that.

'You're on the wrong side, mate,' Al told him.

'I've got a job to do,' said the kid.

'So've we, if they'd let us do it,' I yelled.

'No one's stopping you. The coach is laid on.'

'Yeah, for how long, though?' I said. Anyhow, Al got talking to the copper and a few days later, he turns up one day on the picket with the rest of us.

'I thought you had a job to do,' I said to him.

'I have, but this is my spare time. I can do what I want in my spare time, can't I?' he said. Could he f***! Naive little bastard. We never saw him again. He got spotted and whisked away. See? It's more than just a job, being a copper. You're taking sides.

Anyhow, this particular horse and this particular copper who rode him were a pair of right shites together. If you ended up next to them on the picket line, you were going to get hurt – trodden on, kicked, batoned, poked in the eye, kicked in the teeth. Something. So some of us decided it was time to get our own back.

Friday afternoon, on the High Street. They should have been back in their bloody barracks or somewhere, the picket wasn't on until five when the next shift came up. Keeping order, they said. Oh, aye, about six thousand coppers running around the place with nothing to do – bound to cause an outbreak of peace and order, isn't it?

There was a little crowd around the horse, it was outside the supermarket. They were always showing off their bloody horses to the kids and that. I edged up behind while he was leaning across and chatting to some bird. I think he saw us out of the corner of his eye but he never thought we'd try owt on. I had this tin of lighter fuel and I squirted a bit on the horses tail – just a bit, just enough to get it going, like. Then I clicked my lighter.

WHOOOMPH! It went up like a bloody Christmas tree, right up its crack. Perfect. The horse reared up and neighed, the copper was clinging on for dear life and trying to drag the nag round to stop his hooves coming down on the crowd. We were shouting our mouths off.

'Whey-hey, whoa, go on, boy!' we were yelling. Someone slapped the horse on the arse. The copper was spinning round, trying to get control and get a look at our faces at the same time. No chance. It was great. It was only fired up for a moment, I didn't exactly burn a hole in it. It was f***ing marvellous.

Then we heard horses behind us. Just our luck, there was a whole herd of the bastards just round the corner. As soon as they heard the shouting they were onto us. I chucked the lighter and ran for it.

We went bombing up the High Street, trying to get lost in the crowd, but we ran smack into a load of riot police coming the other way. Someone grassed us up, I reckon, they knew there was some trouble coming. We turned off into a side road and ran hell for bloody leather downhill with the f***ing cavalry clattering away behind us.

Have you ever been run down by the cavalry? Don't try it, it's f***ing horrible. Simon James fell, they had him. Whack whack whack. Blood everywhere. Those sticks are bloody great long things, they get a real swing in on them. They don't like you setting fire to their horses, they were really pissed off. We had no chance of outrunning them, so I turned off and dashed in through one of the houses. It was Jeff and Alice Thomson's place. As soon as she saw us, Alice ran through and opened the door at the back so's I could get out quick. Her old man even handed me a biscuit on a plate as I went through, and I snatched it and stuffed it in me mouth as I went, even though I didn't exactly feel like a snack at the time.

Out the other side – and the bastards were waiting for me. They were everywhere! I ran four or five houses down till I got to Jamie's place, banged on the door, it opened, pushed through it . . .

'Go on, man!' yelled Jamie. They were pounding at the door behind us before I even got out of the front room.

F*** 'em!' Jamie yelled. I was out the back already . . . and would you bloody believe it, it was washing day out there. The whole street had filled their yards with white sheets and knickers and god knows what else. I jumped up on top of the outhouse and down into the next yard and up the next outhouse. I could see the police coming down one side of the street. I wasn't far off our place. I could see our Billy standing on another outhouse shouting summat at me. I stopped and had a look around. There were coppers chasing people all over the place, knots of fighting. It looked as though the whole thing had turned into a major confrontation. Then a whole bloody battalion of them turned the corner on their horses and came galloping along towards me. I jumped down and ran through the yard but I got tangled up in a sheet. I pushed me way out of the yard, trying to get the sheet off me face, but it was wet and sticking.

'Tony! Tony! Not that way!' I heard Billy shouting at me, but it was too late by then. The sheet was sopping. I stopped, just for a second to get it loose, and I tripped up. I could hear them coming. I got back up, I tripped again, I got back up . . .

Whack whack whack whack. One two three four. They must have been taking it in turns. And that was about the last thing I knew until I woke up in the cells hours later.

They kept me in overnight to go in front of the court Saturday morning at ten o'clock. They have special sessions to deal with us, they make so many arrests. It's a foregone conclusion, of course. Justice? It's not justice. It's whose side you're on. Whose side are you on, comrade? Ask yourself. Don't bother asking the police or the magistrate. They know very well what they're doing.

They almost had to let me go, actually. The cowardly bastards must have had a go at me while I was out cold, because I was black and blue from head to foot. I could hardly bloody walk. Well, that's usual, but they'd made a bit of a mistake when they batoned me with that sheet over my head. They hadn't been able to see what they were doing, so they got me on the face. The side of my face was out here, black and blue, red and yellow. It was practically green in places. Christ, it was painful. It was gorgeous. Not the sort of thing they like to put up in public. If you get beaten up like that, they usually let you go rather than let people see what they get up to when they've got you on your own, but in my case they wanted to make an exception because of the horse's arse. They love their horses so much, you see. In the end they decided to say that the horse had kicked out at me in selfde-fence. Everyone would feel sorry for the poor horse, no one would blame it. What a load of shite! But it was going to work for them, and they knew it.

My mate Billy Watson got knocked about badly one time – they hated him because he wound them up so much, so they beat him black and blue, but they did it so you couldn't see a mark on him. All on his upper arms, his back and his legs and his stomach. But he got back at them. He waited till they had him up in court, and while the copper guarding him was looking the other way, he wiped off his top.

'This is the side of the story they don't want you to see,' he said. He was a total bloody mess, they'd really gone to town on him. The court-room went really quiet. And guess what? He got let off? The coppers got prosecuted? Did they f***! He got an extra month inside for contempt of court. For taking his shirt off. You have to be dressed proper in Her Majesty's court of law, see.

My case didn't take long. In and out like a dose of salts, I was. If I'd been a big union man they'd have put me away inside, out of the way. But I was just a working man with no work so they fined us instead. One hundred quid. They know we've no money. Just before f***ing Christmas and all. Happy New Year, you bastards! Thanks a bunch. Where were we going to find that sort of money? Eh, with a bit of luck the Miners' Social might help us out – they do with fines quite often. But then again, when they found out why, about the horses arse, maybe not. It's not the sort of public image Arthur Scargill likes for his boys.

Dad and Billy came along, anyhow, to lend us a bit of support. Dad did anyway. From the look on Billy's face he'd've rather have been somewhere else, but I expect Dad made him come. Dad was furious with me, I could tell, but I wasn't in any mood for it and he had the sense to keep his mouth shut. The fact is, I was f***ed. There's no other word for it. There was a little bit of me kept wanting to giggle because of the memory of that horse with its arse up in flames – just a little bit – but the rest of me was just f***ed. They'd done me over good and proper. I was pissed off for getting caught, I was pissed off for being beaten to buggery by the police. I'd spent a night on a concrete floor in the cells, getting woken up every half an hour for a 'safety check', and I'd been charged a hundred quid for doing it. I was depressed, if you want another word. I felt about half an inch tall. I felt like a piece of dirty little shite.

We caught the bus back and came up the road with the sea at our backs, up to our road, the three of us together. I just wanted to get to bed and weep my heart out like a little kid.

And you know what? It still hadn't finished. There was this woman waiting there, outside the house. I'd seen her somewhere before, god knows where. She seemed to know our Billy, though.

'What's going on, Billy?' she asked.

'Please, miss, don't,' he said.

'Where were you?'

'Our Tony was up in court, I had to go,'

he hissed. 'I tried to ring you, miss, but you weren't in.'

'Who the f*** are you?' I asked her. I looked at Dad.

'I think we'd better all go inside,' he said.

So we trooped in. I was looking at Billy. Was he in trouble? Because I was going to bloody leather him if he was. We've got enough on our plates without some middle-class bitch poking her nose around.

'Have you been mucking around at school?' I asked him.

'Get off!' he said.

We got into the front room and turned to face her. She sighed and crossed her arms.

'I know this might seem difficult for you,' she began, 'but today Billy has missed an important audition.'

'What?' I couldn't believe me ears. 'Audition? For what?'

'For the Royal Ballet School.'

'The Royal Ballet?'

I could not even begin to imagine this. Here I was, I'd just had the living shite beaten out of me by the bloody coppers, I'd been shat on by the court, I'd been without a wage for over half a year . . . and oh, dear me! Our Billy was missing an important audition with the Royal Ballet School. Dear, oh, dear!

'You got to be joking, though,' I said.

'I'm perfectly serious.'

I looked at Billy. 'Ballet?' I could feel myself going. I was really getting ready to blow.

'Yeah.'

'Whose side are you on?' I asked him.

'It's not a question of sides,' she began. But I'd heard enough. I just went mad.

'Have you got any idea what we're going through?' I yelled, right in her face. I could see her flinch, but she stood her ground. 'And you come round here spouting this shite. Ballet? What are you trying to do, you stupid bitch, turn him into a f***ing scab for the rest of his life? Look at him! He's only twelve for f***'s sake.'

'You've got to start training when you're young,' said Billy.

'Shut it!' I had really had enough of it. I was about ready to take a swipe at the pair of them. 'I'm not having any brother of mine running around like a right twat for your gratification,' I told her.

'Excuse me, it's not for me,' she snapped. She'd gone as white as a sheet. She had every right to be. I was that far off twatting her one.

'What good's it going to do to him? He's just a kid. What about giving him a childhood, eh?'

'I don't want a childhood, I want to be a ballet dancer,' the little bastard bawled.

'Give the boy a chance,' she began.

'And what do you know about it anyhow?' I mean, who the hell did she think she was? What right had she got to come in here like this, offering the Royal Ballet on a plate? 'What qualifications have you got?' I asked her.

'I didn't come round here to defend myself,' she said angrily.

'I think you might be some sort of nutter. I could get the social on you, yer cow.'

'I think you should calm yourself down, sonny.'

Sonny! The smarmy middle-class bitch. I tell you, I was just dying to thump someone. Dad was being his usual useless self, just stood there staring like we'd all turned into blue cheese or something. Well, someone had to tell them what was what. I grabbed hold of Billy. She took a step forward as if she could stop me, but I pushed her back. I picked him up and dumped him on the table.

'Right, you want to dance? Go on then – dance! Come on. Let's see this f***ing dancing.'

The woman took out a fag from her coat pocket and rolled her eyes. 'This is ridiculous,' she hissed, like the poisonous old snake she was.

'Oh, aye? Go on then. If you want to be a f***ing ballet dancer, do it! Let's see yer. Dance!'

'Don't you dare, Billy.'

I'd really lost it by that time. 'What sort of a teacher are you? He's got the chance to dance and here you are telling him not to. Dance, you little twat! No? Right, so piss off! He's not doing any more dancing, and if you go anywhere near him again, you middle-class cow, I'll smack you one. Got it?'

Well, all right. I'm not right proud of meself. I could have handled it a bit differently, but you can't blame me. Give it to her, though, she stood her ground.

You sanctimonious little shit,' she hissed. 'What are you so scared of? That he won't grow up like you to race whippets or grow leeks and piss his wages up the wall? Listen, I've been with him every night for the past two weeks and you haven't even noticed, that's how much you care for him, so don't lecture me on working-class solidarity and the British class system, comrade. Got it? Right, so piss off yourself.' She blew a nice big lungful of smoke at me and gave Billy a nod. 'See you, Billy,' she growled. And she walked out.

'You f***ing bitch!' I yelled after her. Then I looked around for Billy, I needed someone to twat, but Dad was standing in between me and him.

Billy stuck his horrible little face round under Dad's arm. 'F*** you!' he yelled at me, and he turned and ran out the house. I took a couple of steps after him, but Dad moved to one side. In the way again. Always in the way!

'And f*** you too,' I snapped. I pushed him to one side and banged out of the house. 'I'm going down the pub,' I said. 'See you later.'

You'd think you'd get a bit of solidarity in your own house, wouldn't you? It's them I'm doing this for, as much as meself. And if I ever catch him dancing, or if I ever see that horrible old bitch anywhere near him again, I'll smack the pair of them till they bleed.

JACKIE ELLIOT

'And here it is, Merry Christmas,
Everybody's having fun
Look to the future now,
It's only just beg-ah-ah-un.'
Slade

Christmas. The turkey, all the trimmings. The crackers. The port, the brandy, a fridge full of beer. Gin and tonics for the wife. My lovely Sarah. The tree, the fire crackling, the tinsel glittering, the presents all heaped up in coloured paper. Nice and warm inside even though it's cold enough outside to freeze your feet to the ground.

Well, not this year.

They had a do down the Social for the striking miners on Christmas Eve. That's us. A nice big tree, kids running round, Christmas dinner. It was OK if you like your Christmas with about sixty other families. We had a banner up: 'Merry Christmas. Nine months. We shall not be moved.' Too right we shan't be moved, we're all too bloody cold. Then we went home.

All it did for me – this shows you what a miserable old bastard I am – was to make me feel sorry for meself because there was so much more that charity could provide than I could. The house was as cold inside as it was out. I went in and had a cup of tea and before I knew it, I found myself staring at the piano. I should never have done it, I know that. But I just thought – well, at least I'm going to make sure we stay warm this Christmas Day. So I dragged the old piano out into the yard. It's not worth anything, no one plays it anyhow, except Billy used to pick out a tune from time to time, but even he's stopped lately. We're all miserable bastards in this house.

My dad used to say, it warms you twice, cutting wood – once when you cut it, once when you burn it. He knew about being cold, his generation, but I never thought me and my kids would have to suffer like that. Oh, aye, it's a cold house, this one, and not just because the heating's off. We've all grown cold hearts over the last months, and that's the truth.

I can't imagine what it's like for my two lads with no mother. Just me to welcome them back when they come home.

I got the axe from the spare room and I chopped the bugger to pieces. Billy came out and sat in the snow watching me. Sarah used to love the snow. It was going to be a white Christmas. It was going to be a blue Christmas, freezing. I kept having to tell Billy to stay back in case he caught a bit in his eye. The strings were lashing around the place, pegs, bits of metal flying everywhere. I was wrecking the axe. I should have pulled all the metal bits off first but I couldn't bring myself to be bothered.

'Do you think she'll mind?' he asked me. I could have killed him. It was the one thing I didn't want to think about.

'Shut it. Billy. She's dead, isn't she?'

I swung the axe. I could see his nan sitting inside watching. I could do without her and all. There was nothing on her face, nothing you could read anyhow. She was cracking nuts with the crackers and then lining them up on the windowsill. She can't eat nuts, she never puts her teeth in. She hasn't got a clue what's going on. I thought, Lucky for her. Lucky for her!

Well, so we had a nice fire on the day itself. Tony did the dinner, he let Billy have the day off. 'No chores for you today,' he said. The way he gets on at Billy drives me mad sometimes, but he did his best to make Christmas a good one for him. Did all the dinner. Gave him a new pair of football boots as a present.

'Where'd you get those from?' said Billy.

'Don't ask,' said Tony. He gave me a pair of decent slippers, and I didn't ask where they came from, either. And me? I don't do shoplifting. I got Susan Harris to knit jumpers for both lads. Happy Christmas! Nice and thick and warm. You need something like that in this house. She knitted them, I gave them. It was good of her to help.

And then. And then. I was sitting there in my chair. We had the bits of the piano all piled up, it was warm but it gave a lousy fire, all cracking and spitting on the rug. I was watching Billy sitting there watching it burn. And I was thinking of all the things I couldn't give him. No big presents, no bright tree, no, well, no mother. Where was my lovely Sarah now we needed her? And God knows, we all needed her.

Tony came in with the chicken. It smelled lovely. 'Merry Christmas,' he said.

'Merry Christmas,' I said. And I couldn't help – I didn't mean it – I burst into tears. I just sat there and wept and all three of them staring at me, but I couldn't stop myself weeping. I let the tears roll down my face and I let them watch them rolling. I'd just had enough. I've just got nothing left to give.

BILLY

'That was a bloody awful Christmas,' I said.
'Did you not enjoy it, then?' said Michael.
'I've had the worst Christmas I can remember,' I told him.

'That's not so bad.'

'What?'

'Well, you're only twelve, so even the twelfth best isn't too bad, is it?'

'Oh, ha ha,' I said. I was in no mood for jokes.

'Sorry.' He stood up and stared at me with his big eyes. He looks like a bloodhound sometimes with those big brown eyes.

'Here.' He took a bottle out of his pocket and passed it to me. 'Have some of this.'

'What is it?'

'Cider.'

'Where'd you get it?'

'Me dad's got loads in the kitchen.'

'Won't he notice?'

'He never notices. He has gallons. Go on.'

I had a swig. It was sour! 'Tastes of piss,' I said.

'You get used to it,' said Michael. He took it back and had a swig himself.

It made me want to spit. 'Who'd want to?' I said.

'Well, it warms you up, doesn't it?'

'I suppose.'

We stood there, passing the bottle from one to the other.

'You could run away from home,' said Michael. 'You could, I dunno, join a dancing troupe or something.'

'Don't be stupid.'

'Well. Maybe it's all for the best.'

'Why?'

'Well, you won't have to go away, then.'

'F***ing hell, Michael! Anyone would want to get away from this shite.'

We were building a snowman. What else was there to do? The piano was all burned up already. Like Michael said, it could have made music for ever but it didn't make heat for even one day, the house was freezing again. Me dad's a miner and we don't have any coal to burn. Joke.

It was a good snowman, except he was filthy dirty. We'd rolled a giant snow tube all up and down the ginnel to make his body, and then we'd gone up the other ginnel and rolled another one for his head and stuck that on top of the first one – it was enormous, but it had picked up all the mud and dog shit and stuff, so it was filthy dirty. We patted clean snow on all over it to cover up the stains.

By that time my hands were freezing. Have you ever had that, where suddenly your hands are so cold they hurt? I started dancing about and moaning.

'God, my hands, my hands! Ouch!'

'Do you want some more cider?'

'I couldn't hold the f***ing bottle. Ah!'

'Give us 'em here.' He grabbed hold of me hands and stuck them underneath his jumper, right in under his clothes onto his skin. It was lovely and warm, but. Well. You know? We were standing dead close to one another. Michael glanced up and down the road to make sure no one was looking. We were under a streetlamp and we had to sort of shuffle a little bit out of the light, without saying anything.

Then we stood there looking at each other.

'What are you doing?' I said.

'Nothing. Just warming your hands up.'

It felt very warm. It was nice but – I had this feeling it was nice for Michael in another way.

'Aren't my hands cold?' I asked him.

'I quite like it.'

I thought about it a bit and then I said, 'You're not a poof or owt, are you?'

'What gave you that impression?' said Michael. He stood there blinking at me, then suddenly we both started laughing. I mean, was he a poof or owt? Of course he f***ing was! It was funny. Then he leaned across and kissed me on the cheek.

'Just because I like ballet doesn't make me a poof, too.'

'You won't tell anyone, will you?'

'Course not.'

We stood there a moment longer. I didn't mind having my hands there if he liked it, so long as I didn't have to do anything else. I suppose I was flattered really, even though I never fancied him. He was my best friend, Michael. It was nice to be . . . well, nice to be fancied, I suppose.

Then I had a stupid idea. 'Tell you what. Come on.' I grabbed his arm and pulled him away with me to the Social.

MICHAEL

I don't know what Billy was playing at. I suppose he just wanted to dance, he hadn't done any dancing for ages. Maybe he thought he was giving me a treat by getting me to wear one of the tutus that the ballet girls wear. Well, I didn't mind, although if I had a choice, I'd rather have a sharp suit like them Motown singers wear meself. But it made Billy happy, and he needed cheering up, so I did it.

I looked quite good in the tutu. I mean, silly, but quite elegant, really. I can carry that sort of thing off.

'You're the girl,' he said.

'No, I'm not. Just because I might be a poof doesn't mean I'm a girl. It's not the same thing.'

'I don't mean that. I mean, for the dance.'

'Oh. Right.'

We were in the boxing ring, standing opposite one another. Billy made me do some exercises – about the only exercises I'll ever do, I'll tell you that! – and then we did some of the moves.

'Plie,' he said.

'That's French,' I said.

119

'I know that. Second and down. And first. Fifth. Up. And one and two. That's it, you're not bad, for a poof.'

'Piss off.'

Off he went. His eyes half closed and he was off somewhere I can't follow him. I felt jealous, actually, because I know there'll never be anything that makes me feel like that. And I was jealous as well because I wanted him to dance with me, and really he was just dancing by himself. I was just someone to dance around. I just happened to be there.

After he'd danced about a bit, we had a bit of a laugh. We started swinging round on the ropes and pushing one another to and fro on the sliding frames and posing on top of the horse and all sorts. Then, finally, we were standing opposite one another, holding hands and looking into each other's eyes – it was just part of the dance, it didn't mean anything, you know? And then I heard a noise and . . .

Christ!

It was his bloody dad.

Listen. Everyone knows Jackie Elliot. You wouldn't want to cross him. He chopped up Billy's mam's piano just to keep the house warm at Christmas. He's a really hard bastard. And there was me, dressed in a tutu, holding hands with his Billy and gazing into his eyes like a bloody . . . well. You know. Like a bloody poof. I was out of that ring and in the corner and the tutu was off before you could scratch your ear. I thought, run for it, Billy . . .

But Billy wasn't going anywhere. His dad looked like he was going to pass out. He was pulling these faces and rolling his eyes. I'd've run for it but Billy got down out of the ring and walked up to him.

'Dad?' he said. His dad just put his hands to his face, in a kind of oh-my-god gesture. I could see everything from where I stood. But Billy – oh, I was proud of him. He never even glanced round. He set his face. And he began to dance.

Man. I hadn't seen it all before, just bits and pieces. It was what he'd been doing with Mrs Wilkinson and it was – well, it was just something else. He was f***ing brilliant. F***ing brilliant. There's no other word for it. Old Jackie Elliot just stood there watching and Billy tapped and leaped and spun and danced like he was on fire. It went on for, I dunno, five minutes or so, and all the time Jackie stood there like a statue. I bet he'd never seen anything like that before. I know I hadn't. I wanted to shout out, 'Hey, man, look at your son! Isn't he just amazing!'

When he finished, Billy was just a few feet away from the end of his dad's nose. He stood there and stared at him. I didn't know what was going to happen. I thought his dad might lift off and hit him but they both just stood there staring at each other. I didn't know what to do, but I did it without thinking – I started to clap. I clapped as hard as I could. Mr Elliot looked at me like it was the first time he realised there was anyone else there, then suddenly he swung round on his heel and walked out. Billy glanced at me and ran out after him.

I went to the window to look out, but I couldn't see much. I caught sight of Mr Elliot going down the road, he was going so fast he was practically running. Then the door banged. I couldn't see Billy but I could hear him.

'Dad!' he yelled.

'Go home, son!' yelled his dad. He didn't even stop walking, just yelled at him over his shoulder. Then he disappeared out of sight. A minute later, Billy came back up.

'F***ing hell,' he said.

'You better go back home like he said,' I told him. 'He's gonna kill you.'

JACKIE ELLIOT

I practically ran down that road. I felt like crying but I'd had enough of that. I was thinking, I've got to do something about this. I was screwing up my face to hold the tears back.

It's been hard for everyone these past months, but I think most people would agree that the strike couldn't have come at a worse time for me. My wife dead. Two lads to bring up on me own. Tony running wild. The wife's mother living with us, half off her head. And Billy. Well, no one really talks to me about Billy. They just look at me and smile. What can you say about our Billy? He's all half-cock and up in the air and – and, well, he's our Billy, that's all.

But there was something else to say about our Billy that I hadn't realised, and it was this. He was bloody good at something.

Now. All right. I don't know anything about dancing or ballet or owt like that, but I've seen it on the telly and I'm just saying that was as good as any of them. Right? And you see, I'd never thought about it. I never thought it was a runner. The Royal Ballet School! I thought it was just that middle-class lass pissing around finding more ways of spending money I hadn't got. But. What if? And then, well . . . why not? If he can do it. If he really has some talent. What then?

My head was spinning. There was nothing I could do about it even if he was Rudolf bloody Nureyev. But see, now. That's not good enough. I mean, if he was good enough to be a ballet dancer, and if he wanted to be a ballet dancer, then I had to be good enough to find some way of making it happen for him. I'm his dad. That's what it's about. Right?

I ran around in the snow on me own like a chicken with no head. I had some thinking to do, and this was how I was trying to work it out. I was thinking, now – what would my Sarah say? She's his mother but she isn't here to help him, so I have to think it out for her. What would she do? Would she threaten this dance teacher with a slap and send her packing? Would she tell Billy that if she ever caught him dancing again she'd smash his face in? No, she f***ing would not. She say, Bloody well done, Billy Elliot, bloody well done! You bloody go fer it! And we'll back you up all the way.

It made me smile, the way my Sarah used to take no shit and I knew for true then that what I'd been doing about it so far was just so much shite. I ran about till me boots were soaking wet and I was just about sobered up – I'd been out for a Boxing Day piss-up with the lads, see. Then I rang up old George and found out where that dance teacher lived, and I went over to have a word.

It was her husband opened the door to me. He stood there swaying and breathing beer on me, then he yelled over his shoulder, 'Is this a friend of yours?' and he walked off without even saying how do you do.

I thought, Bloody middle classes! Who does he think he is?

I went through. She was sitting on the sofa. I got straight to the point.

'How much is it going to cost?' I asked her.

'And a merry bloody Christmas to you too.' She shook her head and sipped her drink. 'Not as much as you might think,' she said. 'Maybe two grand. But there's a good chance the council's got some scheme or other.'

'Two grand? I was . . . well, I was thinking of just the audition.'

'The audition? Oh, I see.' She laughed. 'Well, it'll have to be in London now, he's missed the ones in Newcastle. It's just a question of the fare down there and somewhere to stay. Look, if it's the fare I'll give you the money.'

I'd been in there not five minutes. 'I didn't come here to be patronised,' I told her.

'Oh, no one's trying to patronise you. You're being ridiculous.'

'Am I?'

'Yes.'

I walked up and down the room trying to think. 'Do you want a drink?' she asked, trying to be sociable, but I shook my head.

'So, how good is he then?' I said.

She shrugged. 'I dunno.'

'You don't know? What the f***'s that supposed to mean?'

Her husband in the corner woke up. 'That's my wife you're speaking to,' he said.

'You shut up,' she told him. Then she sighed and looked at me. 'Look, I don't want to make any promises, you know? I don't get that many boys, not many do it round here, you might have noticed. But I suppose there's not that much difference between boys and girls at that age and . . . well. Put it like this. Billy's the best I've seen. I've been doing this for twenty years now. And he's the best.'

'The best?'

'Oh, yes.' She nodded. 'I don't *know*, but if you ask me what I *think* – and it's just what I think – then I'll tell you.'

I nodded.

'Well, I think Billy's brilliant.'

It was obvious she didn't want to take any shit. That was good enough for me.

'Thanks for all you've done for him. But he's my son, isn't he?'

'Oh, aye.' She nodded and glanced over to her

husband, but he'd fallen asleep. She smiled at me. 'Great, innit.'

I thought, at least she's got one. A partner, I mean. A spouse. But then, looking at that fat piece of shite in his armchair, I thought, maybe I was better off than she was after all.

Outside on the road again I didn't stop thinking. It was freezing cold, my feet felt like blocks of ice. I went out to have a few jars on me own before I went back. The lads were in bed at home. I went in to have a look at Billy, just to remind meself who he was. I was thinking – the best? Our Billy? Cackhanded, silly Billy. That's what his mam used to call him when he was little. He was always dropping things. Our little Silly, she used to say. I sat down on the bed next to him and he woke up, but I just put my hand on him and pushed him gently down onto the pillow.

'Go to sleep, son,' I told him. I sat there listening to his breathing. He was my son. He was Billy Elliot, that's all. But maybe . . . well, maybe he really was brilliant at something as well. Maybe he had a gift. And what was I going to do about it? I needed money. The trouble was, see, I'm not the best at anything, certainly not making money. All I know how to do is dig coal up out of the ground.

If it was anything else at any other time I know what I'd've done. I'd've gone and asked the Relief Committee for help. But what a time to ask for money – and for ballet? Forget it! I'd get laughed out. No one had a bean – not for food, not for fuel, not for a patch to mend our old clothes. The village was half frozen to death. All the wooden fences had been uprooted and burned, sheds and houses and even the little bandstand in the park had been taken down and burned up. People were going hungry, and I was going to walk in and say, 'My Billy wants to be a ballet dancer' . . . ? I could see it now.

'Aye, and our kid wants a new winter coat but he can't have that, either.'

No chance. I couldn't ask the men to help me out on this one. I had to do it meself.

After I left Billy that night, I went upstairs to my bedroom. Our bed was there still. Me and Sarah. Our double wardrobe had gone, though, I'd put that in the fire weeks ago. All her things were in boxes in the corner. After she died I wanted to chuck everything out, the lot, right down to the bed so I wouldn't have any reminders, but Susan Harris stopped me. She said I wouldn't need any reminders, Sarah'd be on my mind for the rest of my life anyhow, I just had to get used to it. And she was right. I think in the past two years not two hours have gone past without me thinking about what I've lost. What we've all lost.

In the chest of drawers, underneath her underwear – no, I haven't thrown that away either – there was an envelope and in the envelope was where I kept her jewellery.

There's not so much. We were never rich. Her

wedding ring, a couple of gold bracelets, a gold chain, a few other bits and bobs. The ring was the most valuable. I didn't think it was going to fetch a fortune, but I reckoned it'd pay for me and Billy there and back. A hundred quid or so should do it. It'd be enough. There might even be a bit left over to celebrate afterwards, when he got in.

It was the one thing I had left of any value; and it was the only thing I had that I'd sworn I'd never sell, no matter how hard things got. But I had no choice. It wasn't up to me. Sarah was telling me I had to. But I think I must have broken my heart doing it.

THE PAWNBROKER

I knew Mr Elliot. I'd had him in quite a few times in the past few months. A leather jacket, a suit, a watch, some cut glass. People thought the strike was good business for me, and maybe it was, but only in the short term. I'll be honest, I think the miners are misguided, I think Mrs Thatcher probably has the right ideas about the way the future is going. Sometimes hard decisions have to be made, but I don't always like the way she goes about it. This is my community too. In the long run, what good is it going to do me if all the local industry closes down? Poor people don't buy much jewellery and they soon run out of things to pawn. So I tried to give good prices and I kept the interest low as I could for the duration of the strike. People have long memories about this sort of thing around here, and I wanted them to remember that Dainty and Sons were fair about it.

I'd seen an awful lot of jewellery at that time. Chains and bracelets, that sort of thing, I'd been seeing those for months, but the rings only really started to come in as Christmas got close.

Everyone wanted to give their families a good Christmas after going without for so long, and by that time they had nothing else left. They'd been scrimping and saving and selling off the family treasures one by one, and now it had come to this. It was awful – not the sort of thing you want to evaluate in terms of hard cash. People coming in with the pain all over their faces. They were so desperate, they had nothing left, absolutely nothing. Some of them tried to explain it to me, so I wouldn't think badly of them. It was heart-breaking, really. And so unnecessary. It was just a matter of time by then, everyone knew that except for the real die-hards. It was just a question of how much Scargill was prepared to let them suffer.

I'd never seen it before, the wedding rings. The odd one or two of course, but never like that, half a dozen a day or more for a while. People had never been that poor before, not in my lifetime. In they came, husbands and wives, singly or together, and they'd put their little band of gold down on the counter and look at me, and my heart just sank every time. I knew I was bound to disappoint them. The thing is, people can't separate their feelings from the pure value. Your wedding ring is your romance, your marriage, your kids – everything. You've probably been thinking about it for weeks, plucking up courage, steeling yourself for it, trying not to think of all the memories it represents, all the love and heartache. But to a jeweller, you see, it's just a piece of gold. It might be worth the world to you, but to me – well. My scales only measure the weight, put it like that.

Like I say, I'd seen Mr Elliot a few times before. I've come to be a bit of a judge of character. People get excited at times like this – violent even. I've been threatened more times than I can count. Not that I think Mr Elliot was going to do anything rash, but I could tell at once that this was costing him dear. If I'd known at the time that his wife had died a couple of years ago I might – well, I don't know what I'd have done. He was a man right at the end of his strength. He needed that money badly, very badly indeed, I knew that. Why else should he come in to sell his wife's wedding ring now, of all times? He'd got through Christmas, which was when people usually reach out and cash in the very last whisper of wealth. Why was 5 January any different? Something must have happened. He really needed that money.

'How much?'

'Are you sure about this, sir?'

'I know me own mind. How much?'

Well. What could I say? People come here for money, not advice. I picked it up, checked the hallmark, weighed it out. Went through the other bits one by one.

'I can offer you twenty-five pounds for the lot.'

'What?'

You see? I watched the colour drain from his face. 'That's my wife's ring,' he said.

'You bought it new? Jewellery is always worth less second-hand.'

'But inflation . . .'

'I'm sorry, sir. I know it must be worth more to you and your wife than I can offer.'

He looked shocked. No, not shocked. Horrified. 'Are you all right?' I asked.

'What?'

'Mr Elliot? Are you all right?'

'Aye.' He looked down at the tinkle of gold. What could I do? It was tat, more or less. 'Twenty-five pounds?' he repeated. 'Make it thirty.'

'Mr Elliot, I wouldn't argue about your wife's ring. I know it must mean a great deal to you, but in purely financial terms, twenty-five is already more than it's worth.'

'Aye. Right.' He stood there looking at it, frowning as if the ring had tricked him. 'OK then.'

'You want to go ahead?'

'Aye.'

'Are you sure?'

'Aye. I'm sure, just give us the money.'

If he'd asked my opinion I'd have told him that a measly twenty-five pounds wasn't worth what it was costing him to do this, but like I say, people don't come here for advice. In fact, advice about that sort of thing is the last thing anyone wants from a pawnbroker. I counted out the notes and handed them over. Before he left

I promised to keep the ring safe until the end of the strike.

'It's just surety for a loan,' I told him. But you could tell from his face, the way he felt, it was like I'd just told him he was tat and that his love for his wife was tat, too. Well. Hard times. No one loves a pawnbroker in times like this, but everyone ends up in my shop. I just hope whatever he had to spend the money on was important enough, that's all.

JACKIE

I don't know how to describe how I felt. It was like being blinded. Like the last little corner of light had been taken away from me. It was like all the good years, before Sarah was taken from us, like they were all worth nothing as well.

Aye, well, I know it's stupid. It was just a ring, but I felt so helpless. I walked out of the shop and I knew at once what I was going to do. And I knew it was impossible to do it, and I knew that I was going to try and do it as hard as I could – for Sarah, and for Billy. Tony? I didn't even dare think about him.

The strike was over in all but name. We all knew it. We had nothing left and the government was still as firm as ever. The strike hadn't spread the way we'd hoped, the public was sympathetic to us, but that's all. Sympathy doesn't win that sort of struggle – you need hard support. There was charity but not much else. Not enough of it, anyhow. A couple of months, maybe even a few more weeks and we'd be called back to work. But it'd be too late by then. The audition would be over by then. And all I needed was one week's work. One wage packet. It's all I wanted, you understand – nothing for myself. I just wanted to give Billy his chance, and I knew that no one else was going to do it for me. I had to sort this out by myself.

It was just a blur, the whole thing. Meeting the others on a patch of waste ground. Gary Stewart was there, I remember that. 'Well, who's the big man now?' he said. I said nothing. Well, he was right. Getting on the coach. They treated us like dirt, counted us off one after the other. You, name? You, not seen you before. Come to your senses at last, took your time. Didn't even let us smoke on the coach. Aye, no one has any respect for a scab, not even the bosses.

I knew news was going to get out. Jackie Elliot's turned scab. Well, sooner rather than later. I didn't try to hide my face like some of the others. I just sat there. Let them see, I thought. And I wasn't going to try and explain it away, either. I knew what I was doing and why I was doing it. I was scared, though, I don't mind admitting that. As we got close to the pit we could hear the roar. The crowd! Yelling and shouting, the police banging their shields, the men chanting. Our bus was second in. I watched the first one slow down and go into the crowd like it was being swallowed up. The men heaved forward, the coppers linked arms and shoved back. The noise was deafening. It felt louder on that bus than it ever had when

I was on the ground. Missiles flying through the air, eggs, stones, bricks, flying over the coppers' heads, crashing against the wire mesh over the windows. The men pushing forward, trying to shove the police right up against the coach and make it stop like that.

Then we went in. My heart was going like a drum. The coach slowed right down. I tried to keep my face forward, I didn't look away. Let them see me, I thought.

We inched our way in. There was this sea of faces and noise all around us, it was terrifying. BANG BANG BANG! Rocks against the grid over the windows. Terrifying. Screaming and shouting. Then a group of men got up and managed to rip the grid right off – god knows how. The window was bare. There was a huge cheer. Straight away stones started coming thicker than ever and the glass cracked and crumbled onto us. Those of us on that side got up and went across to the other window. The coach had stopped by this time and the crowd was rocking it from side to side and my heart leaped, but it wasn't fear. Understand? I thought, Good. Because, if they turned it over and pulled us out and kicked us to bloody death, that way I wouldn't have to go in. I wouldn't have to go through with it. I wanted them to get me. I wanted them to know what I was doing.

The police were lashing out, men were going down. The coach inched forward. I turned my head to one side to look out of the window next to me, and what did I see, staring straight back at me? Our Tony. Right there. Our eyes right into one another. The coach moved away in through the gates. I felt like I'd turned to stone. I'd thought I didn't care who saw me. I'd thought nothing mattered any more, but when Tony watched me riding the coach in through the gates to the pit, I thought I was going to die of shame.

TONY

I cried out, 'Dad, Dad!' The coach pulled away and through the gates as if my voice had scared it off. Just for a second I wished I'd kept my mouth shut and I looked from side to side to see who else had seen. But then, well. The look on me dad's face. I never saw me dad look like that at me. He was like, like a kid about to burst into tears. Like he was dying. I just had to get to him, that's all I knew. I shoved me way through the crowd and ran round the wire to the side, and I wasn't thinking then about what a traitorous bastard me own dad was, I was thinking – no, I knew – I knew he was in trouble. I was scared for him.

I ran round the fence. I could see the scabs getting off the coach, I was hoping it was a dream but there was me dad with them. I bawled, 'Dad! What the f*** are you doing! Dad, come back, Dad!' He heard me, looked over to me. The official tried to shunt them inside out of sight, but Dad pushed him away and took a few steps towards me. The official grabbed him, and Dad swung at him, but it wasn't much of a punch, it was a sort of lunge, like he was drunk or mad or what. And he was crying. Crying. I never saw me dad in tears before. I screamed 'Dad! Dad!' over and over, and he came staggering towards me. It was terrible. That f***ing wire! He came right up to it and leaned against it, and I was trying to put my hands through to touch him. I wanted to put my arms around him. He was leaning against it, tears pouring down his face, barely able to say a word.

'It's for wee Billy,' he said.

'F*** Billy! You can't go back, not now!'

'Look at the state of us, man! What have we got to offer the poor sod?' He was a right mess, all snot and tears, and I was f***ing crying now and all. What a pair! I couldn't help it. It was my dad, see?

'You can't do this, not now. Not after all this time. Not after everything we've been through.'

'He might be a f***ing genius for all we know,' he said. He stood back and wiped his nose, a big trail of slime up his arm. I just wanted to take him in my arms and tell him it was all right, everything was gonna be all right. I never knew! I didn't understand.

'Please, Dad!'

'I'm sorry, son. I'm sorry.'

'Dad, please . . .'

'We're finished, son. What choice have we got? Let's give the kid a f***ing chance, eh?'

'He's just a kid, he's only twelve years old, for

Christ sake! What about me? You can't do this. We'll find him some money if it's that important. We'll get him some. just come out, Dad. Please! Do you think he'll be proud about this, do you?'

Some people ran up behind us. Robert Martin and Colin Simons from the union. 'What's he playing at, Tony?'

'It's all right, he's coming back out. Aren't you, Dad?'

Dad just leaned there, tears and snot streaming down his face, saying, 'I'm sorry, I'm sorry, I'm sorry,' over and over.

'Just get him out of there!'

'Aye. I will. I will.'

And I did get him out. He was in no state to work, even the bosses could see that. They didn't want someone having a nervous breakdown all over the coalface. Bad for publicity. They let him out the back way, away from the big crowds. It was in their interest as much as ours. Later on, in the parlour drinking tea, he tried to explain it to me, but he didn't make all that much sense to me, to be honest. He was never all that good with words, Dad, and just then he could hardly get the words out. I'd have thought he was drunk if I didn't know him better. But it gave me food for thought all the same. That stuff about Mam. That was true – she'd have let Billy dance. She wouldn't care who thought what about it, and like he said, she certainly wouldn't have let me kick his dance teacher out of the house like that.

Well, I was a bit over the top that day, but you couldn't blame me. Seeing my dad like that made me feel different. You know? You always think your dad can cope, that he's in charge. Like, your dad always knows what's what, what to do, how to do it. All right, I'd been pissed off with him lately for being a useless old bloke, I didn't like the way he was and all that. But he was still Dad, he was still responsible for things. Now it looked like he wasn't any more. And that meant, somehow, that I had to be. I had to step in to sort that sort of thing out. It makes you think.

But. But. What a bloody time for him to crack up! What a bloody time for Billy to decide he wanted to ballet dancer! Well, I promised I'd help, but it's one thing to say Billy's allowed to dance. It's a whole bloody thing else paying for him. How the f*** were we gonna manage that?

GEORGE

I said, 'Ballet?'

'Ballet,' said Tony.

'Tony, man.' I looked across at Jackie. 'You are f***ing desperate, aren't you?'

It was in The Bell. The two of them sitting there. Jackie looked like he'd lost about a stone overnight, totally washed out. I think he was having some sort of a nervous breakdown. As for Tony, well. I suppose he knew what he was doing. But he didn't look all that happy about it, that's all.

'You've done it before,' said Jackie.

'Aye, for boxing or sport, like. But ballet?'

'Why not ballet? If he's got the talent.'

'Has he?'

'Aye, he has,' said Tony.

'Who says so?'

'Well, I say so.'

'I went round to see his teacher,' said Jackie. 'Mrs Wilkinson.'

'She says he's good enough. She says he's the best she's had.'

'Well, she should know, she's been doing it for long enough.'

'That's good enough for me, then.'

'Will it be good enough for everyone else, though, Jackie, man?'

'That's what I want to find out.'

I looked across at Tony. He shrugged. 'We've got to try, man. It's better than the alternative, like.'

'You'll excuse me for saying so, Tony, but you don't look all that convinced yourself.'

He shrugged again. Jackie glanced across at him.

'He should have his chance, that's all,' Tony said.

I finished off my pint and Tony got up to get me another. I put me hand on his sleeve. 'All right, Tony, you don't need to bribe me,' I said. It was just a joke, but he practically hissed back at me.

'It's not a bribe, man, it's a pint.'

'Aye, and it's my round. All right?' I shook my head at jackie. 'I never thought I'd hear you telling me you want your boy to be a ballet dancer, that's all.'

'Well, it's what his mother would have wanted, George, so I have to think for her now she's not here.'

'So that's all there is to it, right?' said Tony. That's Tony – angry as ever.

'Right. OK then.' I got in another three pints and brought them back to the table. We sat there a while sipping away.

'Well, it's not going to be easy, is it?' I said. 'People have got no money left for food for their own bairns, let alone –'

'Do you think I don't know that? This isn't easy

for me either, George. But it's like Dad says. Our mam isn't here any more, so we have to do what she'd have done. Do you think she'd have just sat down and told him no?'

I knew Sarah. Well. He had a point there. There wasn't a woman like her for sticking up for her own.

'Would she f***,' said Tony. 'So. We have to be Mam for her. Right, Dad?'

'Right, son.'

'So, then.'

Well, maybe. And maybe Sarah would have stood a chance.

'OK then. We'll make a go of it.'

'Good man!'

I nodded, but between you and me, I thought we had about as much chance of selling Maggie Thatcher's knickers at auction as we did of getting folk to part with good money to send Billy Elliot to ballet school that winter.

Business done, Tony couldn't get out of there quick enough. He downed his pint, wiped his mouth and got up.

'See yer then, George. I'm off down the Social. Meeting this afternoon. Keep an eye on Dad, will you?' He waved his hand over jackie's head as if he was asking me to take care of his kid rather than his dad.

I nodded, and he cleared off. Me and Jackie sat there and finished off our pints, then I got another couple in. We settled in to a bit of a session after that. It was on me. I mean, if you can't buy a friend in trouble a few pints, what use are you? It was good for him. It was either five pints down The Bell or up to the doctor for some pills, and I know which I'd prefer. We got tiddly quick. He told me about trying to sell the wedding ring and, well, I think I understood then why he'd done what he'd done. Because, you know, jackie and Sarah Elliot, it was a real love affair. They adored each other. He used to say to me, when he'd had a few, that he couldn't understand how someone like him had ended up with someone like her, he felt that lucky. Oh, I envied him. I wish I felt like that about my wife. So. He's had a hard time these past two years. You can understand it. He must have felt so lonely. He must have felt that he had nowhere to turn.

I had something else on me mind I wanted to clear up but it took another two pints before I plucked up courage.

'Jackie, man,' I said at last. 'Your Billy.'

'Aye?'

'You know.'

'Know what?'

'Well, ballet and all. It's a bit . . . isn't it?'

'A bit what?'

'Well.'

'Go on.'

'Do you think he's . . . you know?'

'What? Out with it then.'

'Oh, f***'s sake, Jackie, do you want me to say

146

it out loud. I mean! Ballet, it's not what most boys round here do, is it?'

'Just because he likes ballet.'

'Aye, all right, just because he likes ballet. But . . . is he?'

'No, he's f★★★ing not.'

'How do you know?'

'I just know, right?'

'How do you know? How can you tell?'

'I just do, all right?'

Jackie was looking at me, half smiling. I was relieved actually, because I thought he might be cross. But he knew what I was on about all right. He was just stringing me along.

'Magazines,' he said. 'Under his bed, like.'

'What sort of magazines?'

'What sort do you think I mean? Sex magazines. Girlie mags. Fanny mags. You remember that sort of thing, George, don't you?'

'All right, all right. Well. Where's he get them from, then?'

'From under Tony's bed, I expect. Quite a good supply.'

Well, I'll tell you, it was a big relief. At least I wasn't going to be raising money to send the lad away to go poofing in London. I leaned back and smiled. 'Well, that must be a relief to you, then.'

'Listen, man.' Jackie leaned forward, and I knew I'd said the wrong thing. 'I don't care what he is, he's our Billy, and that's good enough for me.

I don't care what he does. He can stuff badgers if he likes, he's still our Billy.'

'Right, OK, message received. Well, Jackie, I'll tell you, Sarah'd be proud of you, that's all I can say.' And I wished I hadn't said that as well, because he sat there in front of me and his eyes filled up with tears.

I pretended it wasn't happening. 'We'll go for it, Jackie. But it's a long shot, man. It's a long, long shot. You know that, don't you?'

'I know, George. But we'll do it. Somehow.'

I thought, You'll be lucky, but I clapped him on the back, lifted up me pint and we drank to our success. And poor old jackie, he just sat there with his pint up in the air and cried, just sat there and cried for all the world to see.

We had a couple of days of putting leaflets through letter boxes, but it was mostly word of mouth. Half the town knew about it by then. Jackie couldn't have made better publicity than riding into the pit on that coach, but if I'd ever thought there's no such thing as bad publicity, I thought different by then. It was nothing new, having a meeting to raise money for some poor kid who had a bit of promise and his folks needed some help. But this was different. We'd never sent someone off to the Royal Ballet School before.

It was a thin turnout on the day, but even so, better than I thought. You had the feeling it was mainly curiosity brought people out of doors,

148

Jackie was sitting by me at the table at the front. I'd had some doubts about it, but he seemed to be getting a bit better, wasn't bursting into tears all the time. Organising the meeting had given him something to do. Tony had hidden himself away in the crowd and I thought to myself, He'll be glad when this is all over, and no mistake. They'd left Billy at home. Didn't want him to see his hopes dashed, I suppose.

I got up and got things rolling. It wasn't easy. The word 'ballet' was sticking in my throat.

'You all know why we're here,' I said. 'And you all know it's a bit different this time. There's a strike on, for one thing, no one has much to spare. We've sent kids away to be boxers and footballers and all sorts, but this time it's Billy Elliot and he wants to be a ballet dancer.'

People were laughing. I gritted me teeth. What else could I do? I'd given me word. I rambled on a bit, then I handed over to Jackie. I was too quick, I know, but . . . well. It wasn't easy, that's all.

Poor old Jackie! Tony should never have let him get up there. He was still a bit dazed, you could see that. I reckon the doctor had put him on pills of some sort anyhow. Everyone was staring at him, and he looked like he was facing a firing squad, not a bloody meeting hall with twenty-odd people in it.

'You all know me.' he said. 'You all know our Billy. You all know George.' He ground to a halt. I nudged him under the table. Gerron with it!

'You all know Mrs Wilkinson,' he said, and they laughed some more. He tried to pull himself together. 'She say's Billy's in with a chance, and I want him to be able to take it if he can,' he said. And then, just as I thought he was getting going, he sat down. Bang.

There was this long pause before I realised that was it. 'Right,' I said. More laughter. It was a farce. I tried to think quick of something to say. 'I've put all the fifty pences in that I take from the boxing. It was Billy or a new punchbag, and Billy's won, and it'll be the first time he's got the better of that punchbag, mind.' That got a bit of a laugh. 'Mrs Wilkinson has put her fifty pences in from the ballet. Now, I have some raffle tickets here.' I waved them in the air. 'We haven't even got any prizes yet, but we will. Anyhow, the prize isn't the point. I want everyone to reach into their pockets and cough up. I know you're being asked all the time, and this is just one more thing and Christmas is only just over. But this is important. Right?'

Everyone began looking at each other. A few got up. No one was moving up to where I was sitting. I reckon they were just waiting for the one to make a line for the door and the whole lot of them would run for it.

'Hang on a minute.'

It was Tony. He was sitting right at the back. I thought, What's he up to?

'You all know me and all,' he said. 'I'm the bloke

150

that set fire to that horse's arse.' Everyone laughed at that. 'We all have to be famous for something. Well, I'm famous for a horse's arse. Billy's my brother and there's been lots of times I wanted to set fire to his arse and all.' They were all chuckling now. I was impressed. He'd set everyone at their ease, which was more than I'd done.

'I know ballet must seem to be a pretty weird thing,' he said. 'I was against it myself for a long time. But. I just want to say this. First of all –' and I saw him looking up and catching his dad's eye as he said it. 'First of all, this strike is about the future. We all know that. My future, your future, your children's future. And that includes Billy's future. Not everyone's going to end up down the pit but they still have a right to their own future, no matter what it is. You can't pick and choose what someone's future is going to be.

'I've been speaking to his dance teacher too. And what she said to me wasn't that Billy is in with a chance. She said he was brilliant. Brilliant. Well, he'll be the first in our family who's been brilliant at anything, except setting fire to arses, so I think he should get his chance. You all know, Billy and me haven't had a mam for the past couple of years. And, well, she'd have wanted this. She'd've let him. In fact, she'd have bloody made him. So. Dig deep. We need your help.'

Yes! How about that. I looked down and you could see how it was affecting Jackie. His eyes had gone all wet, and I could have run over and kissed

Tony for that. Then he was back up again. 'One more thing. George has shown you the raffle tickets. Well, if anyone thinks they sneak out the back without buying one, I'll be waiting for them outside, right? So get your money out, and that's a threat. Right?'

Everyone laughed again. I couldn't believe it, how did he manage to speak like that? Bloody hell. I never knew he had it in him. And what's more, it had done the trick. Everyone was up and shuffling towards the front to get their tickets. I sat down and started writing down names and addresses, but I had half an eye on Jackie and Tony. Jackie jumped up as soon as he could and pushed his way back to his son, Tony pushed his way forward to his dad. They just stood staring at each other while people went past them – most of them forward, some on their way out.

'Well, I only f***ing said what I thought you were going to say, you daft f***er,' said Tony. 'I thought you were going to but you just stood there like a bloody twat. I had no choice, did I?'

Jackie didn't say owt. He just stared at Tony and nodded, once, hard. And Tony nodded back, once, hard. They were staring into each other's eyes. And then Jackie nodded back at him. And then –

'Give him a f***ing hug, you stupid bugger!' someone yelled out. And while everyone was politely looking the other way and getting out their pennies, Jackie and Tony Elliot had their arms round each other at the back of the hall, hugging

152

and banging each other on the back, and crying their heads off for all I know. See? A strike like this breaks some families in half and it brings some together. But I never thought I'd see Jackie and Tony come together over ballet dancing, I'll tell you that for nothing!

BILLY

And the next thing I knew, I was on the bus to London. It was a roller coaster. One minute I was some sort of weirdo and the next thing I was having raffles and dances and fundraising done for me. One minute I was letting the side down and the next thing, Dad was rifling through the drawers looking for things to sell. Even Tony was going round selling raffle tickets and the like. It was real nail-biting stuff. We had to have coach fares for me and Dad and B&Bs and a bit more to spend on food and the underground train. It was touch and go for a long time. Right at the end we had to cancel a dance at the Social because the heating broke down and we thought we'd had it. I really did think I wasn't going to go, but then Dad found some money from somewhere. I don't know where, he never told me where from.

Anyhow, it was on.

I rode down on that coach, and it was so exciting . . . all the way to London. The houses went past and then the fields went past, and then we were already going through towns I'd only ever heard about. Then we went sailing past Durham and . . .

London.

'What's it like, Dad?'

'What?'

'London!'

'I dunno, son, I never made it past Durham.'

'You've never been, like?'

'Why should I want to go there?'

'Well, it's the capital city.'

'Well, there's no mines in London,' he said.

'Christ, is that all you think about? Mining?' I mean! I used to think he knew so much and here it was, I was only twelve and I was going to London and he's forty-five and he's never even been south of Durham.

It took ages. When we got there, I wasn't terribly impressed with it at first. It was just houses – bigger houses than I knew but nothing that special. But then it just went on and on. It was huge, it was more like a whole county than a town. It went on for ever, houses and streets, and then more houses and more streets. And all the time the houses got bigger and higher, three storeys, four storeys, five storeys high. Me and Dad were peering out the window like a pair of kids. I was impressed then all right, and I didn't know it but I hadn't seen nothing yet.

Our B&B in Victoria wasn't much. I've had better eggs and bacon in the morning and all.

'We could give them a few lessons in how to

cook an egg,' my dad said. He was right, but it wouldn't have made any difference if the egg had been cooked by the Queen. I could barely eat a thing, I was that scared. We'd come all this way just for me and all I could think was, How the hell can I dance feeling like this? I didn't stand a chance.

'Are you not going to eat your bacon?' said my dad.

'I'm not hungry.'

He forked it onto his plate. 'We don't want to let it go to waste.' He nodded at me. 'You better have some cereal or something, you'll be wanting some food in your stomach for today, won't you?'

'I can't eat owt,' I said. But he made me eat some cornflakes with loads of sugar on just to keep me going.

Then we caught the tube to the Royal Ballet School. The tube was great, I enjoyed riding on that. When we got out – well. You know. London just goes on and on getting bigger and bigger. The buildings in that part were enormous. Just enormous. And the school itself was so big and posh, all pillars and these huge doors and everything. It was like a bloody mansion or a palace or something. I stood there at the bottom of the steps looking up at it and I could feel my heart just sinking down to me toes.

'Bloody hell,' said me dad. 'Is this where we're sending you? How much is it going to cost to keep you here?'

We walked up the steps. I think they were about the width of our street. And you know what? The whole thing was horrible. It was just totally f***ing horrible. I knew, as soon as I saw that building, I knew we'd made a mistake. No one told me it was going to be like that. I thought it was just dancing. Now I could see why Tony had started off so angry about it, because it wasn't just dancing. It was posh gits. It was bosses and people who don't give a toss about anyone. And me, I'm not a posh git. And I don't want to be, either.

The changing rooms were awful. They were full of these posh kids going, 'Es this youwr fowst thime? Itsth my second thyme, oh, isn't it nerwve-wacking, oh aye say . . .' all lah de dah bom bom.

'I dunno,' I said.

'What?'

'I said, I dunno,'

'Pardon? Sowy, youwr accent. Ay'm Thsimon, by the way. Did yew say yowr name?'

'Billy Elliot, From Everington. County Durham.'

'Duwham? Isn't there suppothsed to be this amazing cathedral there?'

'Dunno, I've never been.'

'What? Pwardon?'

'Just shut it, will yer?'

'Sowy.'

Well, it wasn't their fault. They couldn't make out a word I was saying. I might as well have come from another country. And I was thinking, maybe I did.

Then the medical was awful with this horrible posh doctor.

'Up on the box, William. Bend over. Good. Right down! And up. Up, up slowly, good boy. That's lovely.'

La de dah, look up my arse.

'Head down. Oh, little curvature here, might not be a problem, very small. Come on, keep coming. Right, jump up, William.'

'Billy. Billy Elliot from Everington.'

'Sorry, Billy.'

I couldn't bear it. I felt like a horse or something. They sent me back to wait in the changing room, but I'd already decided I'd had enough. I sneaked out and found me dad waiting at the top of the stairs.

'Have you done? How's it gone?'

'Dad, Dad, I've changed me mind, I don't want to do it, please, for f***'s sake, I've –' He didn't even let me finish. He just grabbed me shoulder and spun me round.

'You come back out of there again, I'll bloody leather you!' He kicked me straight back in and closed the door. I could hear him dusting his palms together on the other side.

And then the audition. It was just pure torture. There was this panel of posh prats, all sitting in a row staring at me, about five of 'em.

'And you are . . . ?'

'Billy Elliot. From Everington.'

'Ah, yes. Now then, to the barre please, Billy. Left arm on the barre. Feet first. Demi-plie, and hold.' And they all peered at me and looked at my legs and my arms and my back and leaned together and muttered like I wasn't even there. It made me feel so stupid. You know, I'd seen some of 'em that was already in the school practising before I went in there, and I knew for a fact I could do as well as any of them if I had the chance, but this . . . it just wasn't fair. You can't dance when you feel like that, you can't do anything properly when you feel like that. If it had been back home at the social with Miss, I could have shown 'em something. Anyhow, they never wanted me there at all. You could tell from the expression on their faces they didn't like me.

Then it was the dance.

'Aye hear you have some mewsic, Billy. You have a pwiece pwrepared?'

Someone turned the tape on. T. Rex. The music came on and right away I knew it was the wrong music for that sort of thing. In that place. It sounded so stupid.

'I like to boogie.

'Jitterbug boogie.'

No, I f***ing don't like to boogie. Not there, anyhow. I just froze. I couldn't move a muscle. It was awful. Someone moved their eyebrows encouragingly – that was about as far towards giving me a boot up the arse as they could go.

I like to boogie.
On a Saturday night.

The music was halfway gone and all I was doing was staring at them. I could feel my chances trickling away down the drain. Then I heard Miss's voice in my ear.

'Billy, you're not concentrating! When you're up there in front of an audience, you have to concentrate, no matter what's going on. So go on – just do it!'

So I just did it. It was a waste of time really, the music was already half done, but I did it anyway. It was over in about half a minute. I looked up and there they all were, sitting there staring at me like someone had just offered them a plum and it had turned out to be dog shit and they didn't dare chew any more but didn't like to say anything in case it was rude.

'Thank you, Billy. You can go now.'

I almost ran out of there, I was so scared. I got back into the changing room and I just wanted to cry. There was just the one kid there, the one who'd spoken to me earlier. I was trying not to show how upset I was. All that money spent on me. All those people running around, leaflets, raffles, dances. Dad rushing his arse off. And I was f***ing it all up!

'Are you awl wite?' goes this kid. He comes up to me. I couldn't bear it! It wasn't my fault, I just wanted to be left alone.

'What's the matter?'

'It was a waste of f***ing time!'

'No, don't be upset. It's just a silly audition.'

'I'm all right.'

'Don't worry, there's always next year.' And then the stupid prat came and sat next to me and put his arm on my shoulder. I'd had enough.

'Piss off!' I yelled.

'You'll be OK –' And I twatted him one. He was bloody asking for it. I got him a good 'un to, right on the gob – smack! Down he went, over the bench. George would have been proud of me.

'You bent bastard!' I yelled. And then of course in they came, all the staff. The people from next door.

'What's going on here?'

Well, and that was it, wasn't it? That kid – I know he was only trying to help, but he should have left me be – he was lying on his back with blood coming out of his nose and his mouth. The only time I land a decent punch in my whole life, it had to be there, didn't it?

So that was that. They were never going to let me in after that.

The last thing was the interview. I don't know why they bothered. Just so's they could tell us off, I expect. They interviewed me and Dad together. Same old shit.

'Mr Elliot, you do understand that mutual respect and self-discipline are absolute pre-requisites of any pupil at this school. Such displays of violence cannot be tolerated under any circumstances. Do you understand?'

Both me and me Dad said yes at the same time.

'We will have to consider this very seriously and it will be bound to affect our final decision. Has anyone anything to add?'

The bloke looked down at the other people on the panel. They were all frowning and glaring at us, but they hadn't got any more to add to that. Well, it was enough. He was more or less telling me I was out.

'Just a few questions, then,' said the tutor. 'Billy, can I ask you why you became interested in ballet in the first place?'

Well, I'd already blown it, hadn't I? It was a waste of time. They all sat there staring at me. Dad nudged me with his elbow.

'Dunno,' I said. 'Just was.'

'Well, was there any specific aspect of ballet which caught your imagination?'

'The dancing.'

I could feel me dad trying not to poke me one.

'He dances all the time,' he told them. 'Every night after school.'

'Yes, we have a very enthusiastic letter from Mrs Wilkinson. She has mentioned your personal circumstances.'

'Mr Elliot,' goes another one of them. 'Are you a fan of the ballet?'

'Well, I wouldn't say I was an expert,' said Dad. That was a bloody understatement.

'You know that pupils who come here must attain the very highest standards, not only in ballet but in their other school work. It's a lot of work. If Billy were to come here, he would need the full support of his family. You are completely behind Billy, are you not?'

Dad looked down at me and then back up. 'Oh, yes. Oh, aye,' he said.

And that was about it. Complete f***ing disaster. The last thing they asked was what it felt like when I was dancing. What was the point? They come from a different planet than people like me and me dad. And anyhow, how can you say something about that – that feeling you get when you forget where you are and what you're doing and even why you're doing it? It just is, that's all.

Then we went home.

JACKIE ELLIOT

The whole thing was dirty from beginning to end. I went with a dirty taste in my mouth and I came back with worse.

There was the money for one thing. Oh, well, it all looked great, didn't it? Everyone rallied round, dug deep into their pockets, shown how the community can overcome its prejudices, even at a time like that. Well, that wasn't how it was at all. I'm not saying people didn't dig deep, but it wasn't enough of them and not deep enough. You can't blame folks. It wasn't quite the fairy tale it looked like, that's what I'm saying.

The money we raised was nowhere near enough. Nowhere near. Ten pences and five pences and fifty pences and two pences – it was a joke. We were dreaming. We were never going to get enough from people who'd been on strike for a year. So. Well. Work it out for yourself.

Tony was out at the time. It was me who answered the doorbell. I never expected it: Gary Stewart, Tony's old mate from school. The one we'd seen in the supermarket that time. The one who asked me who was the big man now on the coach. You know – the scab.

Well, I couldn't afford to be so proud now. I let him in, took him through into the parlour. He didn't sit down. Stood there in the middle of the floor and said he wanted to help Billy.

Well. I didn't know what to say.

He did it quite well, I have to say. He took an envelope out of his pocket, but he never held it out for me to take. He just put it on the table.

'There it is,' he said. 'I know how desperate you must have been to try and break the strike. Anyhow, I reckon he deserves a chance.'

I just looked at the envelope. Fat thing.

'I don't know if I can accept it, Gary,' I told him.

'It's not for you, it's for Billy,' he said. 'Accept it for him.' Then he turned and left, quick as he came in. I let him go out alone. I heard the front door open, then he paused and came back in.

'I want you to know, Jackie, this is between me and you. I won't be telling anyone, not a soul. Even my wife doesn't know about this. You don't have to tell anyone either.'

'Why should I want to hide it?' I asked.

He shrugged. 'Why tell them? It's none of their business. If I'm not going to make a deal about it, neither should you.' I never nodded or anything. He shrugged, turned and left. I heard the door go. I went to sit down. I watched the envelope lying there. After a while I opened it and took the

165

money out and counted it. Fifty quid. It was enough. It was plenty.

I couldn't hide it from Tony. He knew how far off we were, he had to know where the money came from. Of course he didn't want to accept it. I heard him out – scab money, dirty money, all the rest of it – but I knew I was going to use it no matter what he said. I'd already made the decision when I got on the coach that time. What's more, I wasn't going to tell anyone about it either. I'd had enough of doing my dirty washing in public. I'd been through it already. Once was enough. Tony complained, but. In the end, he kept mum about it, too.

So you see, it wasn't like it looked. The community rallied round, everything worked out. No way. It was our dirty little secret, more like. That's how it felt. It was expensive stuff, that money. Billy didn't know, of course.

And then when we got there – poor little bloke! I wouldn't have liked to go through that. And I have to say, it didn't go well, it didn't go at all well. All that effort and heartache and treachery and it was shite and it made me feel like shite and it made him feel like shite too. On the way home I was thinking, Well, it's no surprise really. All those other kids, they had every advantage you could think of. You could tell. Rich parents, good homes, first-class schools. The schools they go to probably cost more than I earn in a year. They were used to that sort of place. What chance did our Billy stand? He didn't help himself, mind – thumping that other lad! In a way I felt proud of him for fighting back, but it wasn't the right thing to do. Not there.

I tried to hide from Billy how bitter I felt about it. Accepting that money. Trying to break the strike. The wedding ring. You can't say I hadn't tried for him. And for ballet! And then, London and their big houses and their posh kids and rich schools. All we ever had in the northeast was our mines and our jobs and a hard life, and now they were even taking those from us. It'd be nice to think they were going to give us something back in return for all those years of hard work, all those lives lost, but when it came to it – no chance.

Back at the house Tony and Nan were waiting.

'We did all right,' I told them, but they could see how we looked, especially Billy. I'd never seen him look so miserable.

'Never mind, Billy, perhaps you ought to get yourself a trade,' his nan told him. 'Something useful.'

'Hush, Nan!' I told her.

'I could have been a professional dancer,' she said proudly. She always says that when you tell her off. But what a thing to say just then!

'How, Billy, we've still got a couple of quid left over. What say we get some fish and chips for our supper, eh?'

'That'd be great, Dad,' he said. 'But I'm a bit tired. I think I'll go and lie down for a while.'

'You go on up, then,' I told him. I looked at Tony, but he shook his head. He was too good for that money to be spent on him.

I could hear Billy crying later. Poor little bloke. I should never have encouraged him. What chance did he stand? Against that lot.

But I got thinking that evening and I decided I wasn't going to give up on him. OK, he'd not done it this time but there was still next year, wasn't there? If he wanted to do it as much as all that, he'd get there. I went up and told him so – I told him I was still backing him up right up to the hilt, and I was expecting my Billy to end up dancing. Anyhow, how did we know for sure he hadn't made it? Those people on the panel weren't there for no reason. They must know what they're up to. If they saw even a little bit of what I saw down the Social Hall that time, or what Mrs Wilkinson saw in him, maybe they'd offer him a place despite him thumping that kid. He'd made it up afterwards, they'd shook hands, he said sorry proper, like. That's what I kept telling myself anyhow, and that's what I told him.

And right at the end of the audition, Billy had said this thing. We were almost on our way out when one of them asked him what it felt like when he danced and Billy . . . well, he's like me, not so good with words, but even so. I really think what he said had an effect.

He said, 'Dunno' – which was what he'd said to

every other bloody question they'd asked him. But then he had a little think and he said something about it feeling like flying. 'It starts off sort of stiff,' he said, 'but once I get going I forget what's going on and I sort of disappear. Like there's fire in me whole body. Like a bird. Like electricity,' he said. 'Yeah. Like electricity.'

I saw the people on the panel glance at one another and I felt a little tingle go down my spine then, because I knew he'd impressed them. Well. He'd impressed me, anyhow.

Maybe they weren't as bad as they looked. Afterwards Billy just wanted to slag them off, but I wasn't having that. I mean, if he did get in, he'd have to mix with them and live with them, it was no good just painting them as black right from the start. When we left, one of them wished me luck with the strike, so he must have been on our side.

'Good luck with the strike, Mr Elliot. I hope you bloody win.' So, see? Even in a place like that there's people supporting us.

It was ages before we got an answer back. I'd just about talked Billy into thinking there maybe was a chance after all, and then I'd started thinking I was doing the wrong thing because he obviously had no chance – you know? I didn't know whether to prepare him for failure or give him hope.

One week went by. Then another. And then the letter came.

His nan got hold of it first. She's only got about half her wits, but she had them all lined up and ready for use that morning.

'Post!' she yelled, and she came rushing in with this beautiful-looking letter. Thick, creamy envelope. She handed it over. I knew as soon as I felt the paper.

'This is it,' I said.

'Open it now,' said Tony.

'Don't be stupid. It's Billy's letter.'

'Aye, and who bloody worked their fingers off selling raffle tickets and all that?'

'Selling raffle tickets, you've forgotten what work is,' I told him, and he grinned at me. Billy was at school and I was dying to have a look myself, but we'd just have to wait. I put the letter propped on the table in between the toast rack and the sugar bowl.

And there it stayed. All bloody day, staring at us. Of course none of us could leave it alone. I kept picking it up. Nan picked it up, Tony did. Next door came round and had a feel to see how thick the paper was. Mrs Johnson on the other side. Susan from up the road. George popped round to have a look. It was getting a bit grubby by then, so his nan decided to keep it clean by hiding it in her pinny and I nearly went mad when I found it was gone. Of course she'd forgotten what she'd done with it and it was half an hour before she found it in there. It was in a right mess by that time. She used to keep biscuits and bits of bread and butter and stuff in that pocket.

'Just bloody leave it alone! It looks like it's been used to butter the toast,' I told her.

When Billy came back from school at four, we were all three waiting for him. I'd booted the neighbours out. This was a family thing. When – I mean if – he hadn't made it this year, he wasn't going to want half the road hanging over him and patting his shoulder telling him not to worry and that.

The door went. As soon as we heard it we were all like kids, rushing around finding somewhere to sit so we were all in our places looking cool when he came in. The door opened. There he was. I looked up at him. I looked down at the letter. I looked back at him. He was still staring at it.

He walked over and picked it up. No one said a word. It was awful. He walked around the table. I could see Tony nodding at him: Go on, open it then. Billy licked his lips. He walked round the table to his nan's room. He pushed the sliding door open and gave us a quick glance, sort of saying sorry. I don't blame him, but I could have killed him. He went inside and closed the door.

And then nothing. Nothing. On and on, nothing. We could hear the paper being opened. We could hear the letter coming out. There was a long pause while he read it. He knew whether or not he'd got in. We didn't.

Nothing. More nothing.

'F*** this,' muttered Tony. He jumped and went to the door, and I only just managed to push in front of him. Billy was sitting in the chair by her bed. He looked up. He was crying. I thought, Oh, Billy.

'Well?'

'I got in,' he said in a tiny little voice.

'YEEEEEEEEEEEEEESSS!' You could have heard the roar from me and Tony halfway up the street. I snatched the letter off him and read it. YEEEEEEEEES! We jumped and shouted. F***ing hell! He got in! He f***ing got in!

'He is! He is!' I kept shouting.

'Is what?' yelled Tony.

'F***ing brilliant!'

The neighbours came running round. Nan was running about kissing evedryone. Tony put Billy on the table and told him to dance and he bloody did it this time. I gave him a big wet kiss right on the smacker and I went running up the road. I had to tell the lads. He'd done it. Jesus! I couldn't believe it. I had the letter in my hand.

'We are delighted to inform you . . .'

I ran up the road as fast as I ever ran anywhere, up the hill into the Social. All the time I was thinking, Our Billy, he's better than any of them posh twats, he got it! I banged the door open to the bar and . . .

'HE'S IN! HE F*** ING DID IT!'

Silence.

'Haven't you heard, Jackie, man? We're going back.'

'What?'

'It's over. The union's caved in.'

'We lost. Back to work on Monday.'

So that was it. It wasn't such a big celebration after all. The end of the strike overshadowed everything. We lost. I remember thinking, Well, at least I'll be able to pay for the ballet school now.

It's a long time ago now. We lost. Thatcher won. I expect that got her a few more votes at the next election, and the one after that, too. And by the time the Labour Party got back in, they were all Thatcherites too, so it's just never stopped since, really, has it? The mines all closed, one after the other, just like the union said they would, just like Thatcher swore they wouldn't. Here in Everington we were lucky, our mine lasted longer than most, but it's gone now, too. The place is like a ghost town.

It was straight back down. Into the cage and down into the pits where the coal was waiting for us, like it always had. And it's still down there, but what's left will stay there now. It's too deep and the veins are too thin. The shafts are all flooded anyhow. That's it for mining in this country. At the time I remember thinking, Well, we lost our future, didn't we? Oh, I know the town will go on, but it won't be the same, not without the mine. It was there long enough for me – I was glad to stop working when the time came – but Tony's been out of work for three years now. We lost that future – but we won another future – for Billy. And that's something, isn't it?

BILLY

'One and two and three and four and up. And hold.'

It was just the same.

'Beautiful necks. Jona, that's not a beautiful neck, is it?'

Drifts of fag smoke floating in front of the windows. Mr Braithwaite thumping away on the piano. It was like she'd been doing this for about three thousand years. Then she spotted one of the girls watching me, looked over her shoulder and saw me.

'OK, girls, practise your plis.'

She came wandering over as if I was there by accident.

'Billy.'

'I'm going today, miss.'

'I know, Debbie told me.'

She sucked on her fag and gazed over at the girls at the barre.

'I'll miss you, miss.'

'No, you won't.'

'I will, miss, honest.'

She sighed. 'Billy, this is when you go out and find life and all those things. And you forget all about me and . . . this.'

'I won't.'

'Yes, you will. Best of luck, Billy.'

She gave me a tired smile, turned and went back to the girls. 'OK, Mr Braithwaite. Heads up. Bottoms out.'

And that was it.

I felt let down. I'd thought I meant more to her than that, after she'd spent so long teaching me for free. Maybe I did. I don't know. You could never tell with Miss.

Anyhow, I had a coach to catch. I turned round and ran home.

'Was she there?' said Tony.

'Yeah.'

'Right. We're off!' said me dad. He picked up one of my bags, Tony grabbed the other. Nan was sat there at the table looking at me out of the corner of her eyes. I didn't know how much she knew. You could never tell with her either. I went over and gave her a big hug and I knew she knew all right, because she hugged me back very tight and wouldn't let go.

'We'll miss the coach,' said me dad. But she just hung on. When she let me go at last, she pushed something into my hand. A five-pound note.

'Nan! That's your pension.'

'That's her pension,' complained Tony.

'Let her,' said me dad. 'It's hers to give.'

I kissed her again, and she hugged me tight all over again and wouldn't let me go.

'We'll miss the coach!'

'Oh!' she scolded him. But she let me go and pushed me to the door.

There'd been a lot of goodbyes. School. I could have done without that. They had a special assembly to see me off, big speech from the headmaster and all that. 'I'm sure we would all like to wish Billy Elliot the very best . . . how proud we are that this school has been able to help . . .' Blah blah blah. What help? No one ever helped me there with dance. I mean, it's OK, no one picked on me or owt, but it was my family and Mrs Wilkinson and the neighbours who did it for me, not the school. I don't remember any raffles there.

And the neighbours and me friends and Michael. And me mam. I went down quite a few times to the cemetery. I went down with Dad with some flowers. Did a bit of weeding and things.

'She'd be so proud of you, son,' said Dad.

I nodded. I was thinking about that time I saw her in the kitchen.

'Shall I tell you something?' he said. 'You know when I changed my mind? Well, it was her that convinced me.'

I looked at him and I thought . . . is it possible? Did he see her too?

'I thought about what she would have wanted,' he went on. 'I thought, What would she say? And I knew I'd been in the wrong. I knew she'd want you to do it.'

'Oh. Right.'

'So you see, that letter she wrote you . . . she is still here watching over you. In some way or other. And she'll be watching over you in London and all.'

'Right,' I said. And maybe it was true. Maybe she was there all the time. Maybe when I saw her, she was just reminding me that she really is there, whether I can see her or not.

'So, Dad.'

'What?'

'I'm really going, aren't I, Dad?'

'You're really, really going.'

'I'm scared.'

'That's all right, son. We're all scared all the time. Don't mind it.'

'Well, if I don't like it, I can always come back, can't I?'

'Are you kidding? We've already let out your room.'

'What?' But as soon as I looked at him I knew he was joking, the bastard. I punched him in his ribs and we rolled all round the grave trying to get one another. It was great.

And now, here it was happening. We headed off

178

down the road in a little convoy, Dad on ahead, then me, then Tony. He said he had to follow up to stop me if I tried to run off. We'd just got to the end of the road when I heard someone calling me . . .

'Oi! Dancing boy!' Michael. I'd already said goodbye to him, but he told me he'd be watching out for when I left. He was standing on an outhouse roof. I ran back for him.

'We're gonna miss the coach!' yelled me dad.

'Will you stop being such an old woman?' Tony scolded.

I ran back up to the outhouse, Michael jumped down.

'See you then,' I told him. He didn't say anything, though. He just looked at me. 'You're being a right old woman, too,' I said. I leaned over and kissed him on the cheek, like he kissed me once.

'Eh, man, not here, people'll see, I have to live here,' he said. I just laughed.

'We'll miss the coach!' bellowed me dad.

'See yer,' I said.

'See yer,' said Michael.

I ran back. Dad was practically running down the road, he was so scared we'd miss the bus. Me, I just thought nothing could go wrong now, but he was right to hurry, everyone else was already on board. The driver jumped out and put my bags in the hold, Dad hugged me . . . and I was on. I got the seat at the back, my favourite. Dad and

Tony stood on the pavement outside. I felt like a bit of an arse, watching them wait for the coach to go away.

I'd hardly said anything to Tony before then, but he came up close to the window at the back and he said something.

I said, 'What?' It was funny, you know, because I knew what he was saying by the way his mouth was moving. He was saying, 'I'll miss you.' I just said 'What?' before I had a chance to think.

But he didn't know that. He glanced behind him, all embarrassed, like. 'I'll miss yer,' he shouted.

'What?' I said. The engine started up and we pulled off. I was trying not to laugh. We were pulling away and Tony was yelling, 'I'll miss yer!' I stood up and banged on the window as if I was really desperate to work out what he was on about.

'I'LL MISS YER!' he bellowed at the top of his voice.

So then I pointed and I laughed. For a second he stared at me and then he realised I'd been having him on.

'You bastard!' he shouted. But he was laughing his head off and all. He came running after us shaking his fist and chucking bits of toffee, crisp wrappers and stuff he had in his pocket after the coach.

'You little bastard! I'll kill yer!' Everyone on the

coach could hear him. They were all laughing and Dad was laughing and I was laughing and Tony was laughing. And the coach went round the corner and . . . then they were all gone.

JACKIE ELLIOT

Well, London never gets any smaller. Maybe it's me that's getting smaller. I've been down a few times now and those buildings seem to get bigger every time. It never fails to impress. I feel as though I own a bit of it now, that's all.

I'm sitting in Covent Garden Opera House. You never saw anything like this place. They could build Everington inside here, it's that big. All gold and red and satin and bows. These seats we were sitting in cost over a hundred pounds a go. Me and Tony. Tony still in his donkey jacket and jeans, looking like a miner. Still making a point. Got in for free, mind. Complimentary tickets. Outside above the entrance, in big letters, it says:

'The Royal Ballet Company. Swan Lake. Billy Elliot.'

I'm Mr Elliot. How do you do?

I get Tony to call over one of the ushers, even though the music is just about to begin. I told him, 'Will you tell Billy Elliot his family's here?'

I always do that. I like him to know. Even though he knows already in this case. This is his first lead role. Dancing the lead. Brilliant, see? She was right, all those years ago.

Tony sitting next to me gave me a nudge.

'What?'

'Look.' He was pointing to the bloke sitting next to him. He was one of those London types. He had a purple cloth wrapped round his head and make-up on.

'What?' I said.

'Dad. It's Michael Caffrey. Remember?'

'Michael? Is that you? What are you doing here?'

'Oh, I wouldn't have missed this for the world!'

Tony whispered out of the side of his mouth, 'Told yer.' He did, too. That Michael's a poof if I ever saw one. Tony'd said it half a dozen times as he was growing up. He wasn't the only one, either. Well, he was right there. I reckon we could all see that coming.

He leaned across to shake my hand.

'You must be a very proud man, Mr Elliot,' he said. He'd almost lost his accent. That didn't take long, I thought.

'I am.'

'It's you that's put him here, after all,' said Michael, and no one ever spoke a truer word. I dug a lot of coal out of the ground to put Billy in here, just like my father and his father dug a lot of coal out of the ground to build places like this. There's coal behind everything in this country. It's still down there. We're not.

The lights went down. The music came up. And

a moment later there was our Billy. He ran on, paused . . . and he jumped. I'd seen him do it a hundred times before but this time, on the stage, every eye in the house watching him, all the lights on him, he jumped like a bloody star. I thought he was going to hang for ever in the air. It's marvellous the way they look just for a second as if they're never going to come down and no one – no one, no one, no one – does it as well as our Billy.

When he landed and he spun round to face the audience and I could see him smiling at us.

'Eh up, Billy Elliot!' It was Michael, shouting it out at the top of his voice. I nearly died – you don't do that sort of thing in these places. People turned round, some of them frowning, some of them grinning.

'Go for it, our Billy!' That was Tony. He stood up, cupped his hands, and hollered. Everyone was looking round and smiling now. Well, I couldn't be left out, could I? I stood up and yelled as loud as I could.

'Billy! Billy Elliot! Our Billy!'

And Billy was up there smiling his head off, and then he did that jump again, one more time, even though he wasn't supposed to, even though it bolloxed the music, just for us.